Wood's Wreck

A Mac Travis Adventure

Steven Becker

* * *

Join my mailing list
and get a free copy of Wood's Ledge
http://mactravisbooks.com

Chapter 1

Mac leaned back in the chair, exhausted, wondering if it were really true that if you kept doing the same thing over and over again, you were insane. He certainly felt like it, as he drained the last of the lukewarm water from the bottle and tossed it to the deck in frustration. He looked out over the clear blue water, its ripples reflecting the late afternoon sun, and thought about his next dive. It was going to be the same as the last dive, and the one before that … and the one before that.

For the last week he'd come out to the same spot, anchored in the same place, and dove at least three times every day. And still it eluded him. For years, he had secreted his stash of gold pieces and other valuables recovered from salvage work in a small cavern, concealed beneath three easily identifiable coral heads. It was a well-hidden cache in seventy-five feet of water a couple of miles west of Sombrero Light off Marathon, well away from the tourists who tended to use the mooring balls by the lighthouse. The site was removed from the famous reef surrounding the tower, and deeper than most recreational divers would venture. Even with his experience, he didn't like to dive this deep unless he used Nitrox— a mixed gas that decreased nitrogen in the blood. Because he chose the convenience of his onboard air compressor, the bottom time before decompression stops were required became shorter with each dive.

A week ago, he had come to pull out a few gold pieces to sell. Lobster season had only been underway a month, and so far it was the worst he could remember. He had started the season optimistically, as always, even following the dismal dolphin fish season in the early summer. Now, in the dog days of August— almost a month into the lobster season—he'd had to dip into his reserves to buy fuel.

Reluctantly, he got up and went to the compressor to check the air gauge. The tank was close to its maximum fill of 3000psi. He purged and removed the fill valve and hauled it to the transom, where his equipment lay in a pile on the deck. It would be his third dive of the day and he wondered how badly he was pushing his decompression limits. A trained commercial diver who had years of salvage and engineering work under his belt, he had never used a dive computer. Most of the diving he had done, especially since coming to the Keys in the early 90s, had been working on the bridges connecting the chain of islands and spearfishing the shallow reefs of the Gulf side, usually in less than thirty feet of water. In that depth, you could dive all day without risk of illness or the need for a computer. The more old fashioned dive charts were good enough, and they were ingrained in his memory.

In this case, though, he had to hope for the best. With the help of the app that Mel had loaded onto his phone, he had at least been able to record his dives, rather than wing it. So far there hadn't been any adverse effects that would indicate decompression sickness, but he knew he was playing around the edges.

Fresh tank in hand, he sorted the pile of gear, slipped the BC over the tank, and attached the first stage. He turned the knob and felt the pressure build in the hoses, checked the gauges, and took a breath to test the regulator. With a tired grunt, he slipped into the harness and buckled the straps of the BC. He stood and moved to the transom, went through the small door to the dive platform, and sat with his legs dangling in the water. Seawater swished around his mask and he spat in it, rinsed it again, placed it over his head, and reached for his fins. Fatigued from the earlier dives, he looked down into the water, stuck the regulator in his mouth, gathered the hoses to his body, placed a hand over the mask and regulator, and rolled sideways off the platform into the warm water.

The crystal clear blue of the water, small particles glittering as the sunlight penetrated it, slipped by unnoticed as he descended with one hand loosely gripping the anchor line. When he reached the bottom, he checked his gauges and finned toward the rock pile. Of the three coral heads that marked the cavern, there was only one still standing; another lay on its side several feet away. He knew what had happened as soon as he spotted the third and largest head almost a hundred yards away with an anchor stuck in its side, the cut line drifting in the current. The Danforth anchor, made for soft bottoms, had its points deeply embedded in the coral head. This kind of anchor was well suited for anchoring in well-known sandy bottoms. Not for bottoms that had coral.

With no way to retrieve it, the boater had evidently tried to drive it out, and in doing so, caused the destruction that had collapsed the cavern. This type of anchor was common on vessels here and anchoring in the sand was the least damaging method of mooring a boat, but also the least effective. Besides being small and lightweight the boat anchor didn't have enough line or chain necessary to provide the correct angle to set the hook properly.

Here, the practicalities of the bottom structure, especially on the deeper reefs, didn't allow this. Grapnel hooks, wired upside down with a piece of light gauge wire, was the preferred method used by experienced divers and fishermen. The safety wire was light enough that even if the anchor caught, it would break before destroying the coral. The damage caused by the boater had changed the bottom structure so drastically that he'd been unable to locate his cache.

The first few days he had been crazed, desperately searching the bottom, wasting time and energy. On the third day, he had laid out his search grids and done everything by the book, but still the cache would not reveal itself. This was going to be his last dive before giving up, at least for a while. At some point, you had to move on. Mel had been brutal in her criticism that a land-based safe would have been smarter, but his had been broken into before, and he believed the sea would hide his secrets. Now, she reminded him, with a full week of soak, his lobster traps should be stuffed ... at least in a good year.

He finned through the water, oblivious to the fish, and worked over the same bottom again, hoping for the one little crack that would reveal the cavern. His breath caught—the first sign that his air was about to run out— and he checked his gauges. The air pressure was pegged into the red, and he wondered where the time had gone. Another breath yielded even less air, and he knew he had only seconds to reach the surface. Cursing himself for not checking sooner, he kicked hard and started to ascend.

Where he would normally have used his BC to bring him effortlessly to the surface, he dared not use the extra air. He kicked again and took the last breath before the diaphragm closed for good. The hull was visible above him now, but the clear water was deceiving; it was probably another forty feet to the boat. Breathing tiny bubbles and hoarding the remaining air in his lungs, he kicked harder, knowing he was going too fast, but the other option was drowning.

Finally he broke the surface, spit the regulator out of his mouth, and gasped for air. Without the aid of the BC, he treaded water and filled his lungs several times before swimming to the boat's ladder. With one hand securely grasping the rung, he tried to calculate the dive charts in his head.

Tired and disgusted, he hauled himself up the ladder and dropped the tank on the steel deck. He retrieved his phone from the helm and checked the home screen. Just one message from Mel, wondering where he was. Disregarding the text, he went to the dive app and started to enter his bottom times and depths for the dives today. After a quick calculation, the chart showed him to be right above the red line indicating that decompression would be required.

He debated whether he should get back in the water, descend to ten feet and do a safety stop, but decided against it, rationalizing that the app probably had a pretty large safety factor built in. If he *did* get symptoms of the bends, he knew from experience that he would get a wicked headache and painful joints. Even that would be short lived. He was confident that he hadn't crossed into the danger zone, which would require treatment in a hyperbaric chamber.

He looked around, not wanting to make the run in and face Mel, but at the same time tired of looking at this same patch of water. She was right that this was hopeless. Tomorrow, he would grab Trufante from whatever bar stool he'd spent the last week on, and go pull his traps. The engine idled and the windlass groaned as it pulled the anchor from the bottom. The anchor secured, he pressed the throttles forward and pointed the bow toward an invisible spot between the three antenna the government used to broadcast propaganda to Cuba and the Seven Mile Bridge, its hump clearly visible on the horizon. The deck rumbled as the twin diesels picked up power and, without a look behind him, he headed toward shore.

The bow easily crushed the small waves in its path as the boat ran at 25 knots; well below the maximum speed of 45, but Mac was in no rush. What awaited him was what he had feared for the twenty years he'd been here: Having to scrounge a living from salvage and repair jobs. Fishing and lobstering was more fun when you had a stash of gold for backup, but without that, he was going to have to work for a living. It was almost twenty years ago that he had escaped Galveston and settled here under the wing of a local legend. He and Wood had built or repaired many of the bridges connecting the 120-mile string of islands together, and in the process, recovered relics of past wrecks, some dating to before

Columbus. They had kept their finds quiet, knowing that revealing them would attract every government agency around. And government agencies liked to shut jobs down indefinitely by labeling them archeological finds.

Mel was another problem entirely. Wood's strong-minded lawyer daughter had moved in with him a year ago. There was a deep love and respect there, but she was having a hard time readjusting to the laid-back Key's lifestyle she had fought so hard to escape. Frustrated by DC politics, she'd allowed herself to be convinced to move back to Marathon and give it a shot, but she went from periods of happiness to those of depression, clearly missing the challenge of her work as an activist attorney.

She needed a cause, and had started volunteering for a non-profit in Key West. Friction had started when the group's good intentions conflicted with Mac's way of life. There was conservation and preservation. The former—although sometimes misguided, like in the case of protecting jewfish that in turn decimated the stone crab population—was generally helpful to the ecosystem; the latter shut down the economy, severely limiting the use of the protected areas. This only encouraged poaching, as it forced lifelong fisherman to ply their trade illegally.

The boat crossed into the lighter green water, broken by dark patches indicating the small reefs that dotted the shallows. These passed quickly, and the visibility decreased, as he moved into the deeper channel and entered Boot Harbor. The engines dropped to a murmur as he eased off the throttles. At idle speed, he slipped between the red and green markers, past several gas docks and restaurants, before turning left into a canal. Several houses in, he adjusted for wind and current, eased the forty-two-foot boat up to the dock, and shut down the engines. He looped the stern line around the cleat and tied it off, then did the same with the bow.

The boat secured, he stepped onto the dock and went to the back of his stilt-framed house; the bottom housed an enclosed workshop, while the upstairs was his living area. Without entering he went around the side, smiling as he saw the driveway empty. At least he would have a few minutes of peace before Mel got home.

Back at the boat, he checked the lines, adding a spring line to the bow, and hosed off the deck and gear. Despite his current mood, he knew better than to ignore the effects the sea water would have on his equipment. With a beer in one hand and the hose in the other, he worked slowly, in no rush to finish the task and face tomorrow.

Chapter 2

Mel was watching the one-hundred-gallon saltwater aquarium filled with farmed coral in the hall outside her office when she heard the sound of despair through the open door of the room adjacent to hers. She looked over at the woman with the flaming red hair, who sat and stared at her computer monitor, pounded her fist again on her glass desk and turned toward the window overlooking the Atlantic Ocean.

She turned her attention back to the tank, which distracted her from watching yet another tantrum. She liked the tank and often gazed at it, wondering how much longer she could handle the bipolar behavior of the woman, Cayenne Cannady, and if she could even make a difference here. *She isn't really your boss unless you get a paycheck,* she thought, referring to the pro-bono work she was doing for the non-profit.

Cayenne had to be in her fifties and wore clothes you were supposed to stop wearing in your twenties. Her hair resembled her name, and her parts were not all hers. Mel's attorney friend Keith Fricker said *that makeup didn't hide crazy,* and in this case he was definitely right.

She took her eyes from the aquarium and looked down at the ledgers spread in front of her. They were grossly incomplete, but from her experience most non-profits did not view themselves as businesses, and spent little time or effort on bookkeeping. Even with the sparse information she'd been able to collect she had analyzed the state of Coral Gardens, the non-profit that Cayenne had founded three years ago. The mission was to grow coral on her permitted site, using profits from the sales of their products to aquarium enthusiasts to fund transplants of Elkhorn and Staghorn corals to the reef. Coral Gardens was originally funded by several research grants and a large donation from her father, all of which had been exhausted last year.

Saving the reefs was a good cause, and Mel, having trouble adjusting to the standard Key's lifestyle of rise, drink, rinse, and repeat, was in need of a project; something to relieve the boredom of the mind-numbing routine of island life. She had seen this as worthwhile, offering her legal services to Cayenne in exchange for a desk and a cause to fight for. The concept fascinated her. Growing coral in the same manner as oysters, using ropes and bins to cultivate the specimens.

But the business plan to raise money by selling farmed coral to saltwater aquarium enthusiasts had tanked with the recession a few years ago, and had suffered the same fate as every other disposable income luxury industry. But as Mel went into the books, she began to see cash deposits that mysteriously matched the non-profit's expenses. Many of them were large, and had no explanation. She knew there were no coincidences in accounting, and the books said danger all over them.

What she needed were the tax returns. She doubted Cayenne would do the complicated forms herself, and that meant, at least, that a professional would have reviewed the books.

She looked back at her computer screen, trying to figure out what had gone wrong. The web browser was open to Google Trends and showed that the saltwater aquarium industry had spiked before the recession of 2008, followed by a crash and a flat line at the bottom of the graph. Mel might have been a lawyer, but after helping her father manage his construction business, she knew that sales were king and without them nothing else mattered. Without revenue, it didn't matter how well you controlled your costs.

Cayenne was coming toward her now and she looked up at the fake boobs arriving a few seconds before the rest of her. The woman had on a sundress shear enough to see the very little bit of a bathing suit clearly outlined beneath it. A wide-brimmed hat and sunglasses shadowed her face, the wrinkles and lines covered with a heavy dose of makeup. Someone really should tell her the look didn't work for her, especially in Key West, but Mel averted her eyes instead.

"Hey. You want to take a run out to the farm with me? You've been staring at the computer and those pesky ledgers for hours. You could use a break."

Mel looked back at her. She had no interest in a boat ride to the backwaters of the Keys where the farm was located. She knew those waters all too well after growing up here. Her father had lived his last years on an island close to the farm. But this might be a good opportunity to corner Cayenne and tell her exactly where the business stood. Trying to explain to the flighty woman that this was really a business first and a non-profit second had been close to impossible. Sure, saving the world was noble, but without money there would be no nobility. Maybe now they would get a chance to talk about it.

"Sure. That would be great," Mel said. She got up, grabbed her phone, and started walking toward the door.

"Don't you want to change?" Cayenne asked.

Mel looked down at herself and wondered why most people felt a bathing suit was required gear for a boat ride. The wind and sun would dry her if she got wet. "I'm good."

They left the three-story Victorian house and walked toward Cayenne's Prius, parked in the narrow hibiscus lined driveway separating her's from the other similar houses on the block, their only difference the style of gingerbread and paint colors. They got in the car and Cayenne pulled out of the driveway.

Ten minutes later, they reached the marina, parked, and

walked down the dock to the charter boat. Another expense that wasn't needed, Mel thought as she casually hopped onto the deck of the twenty-four-foot center console. The captain offered a hand to Cayenne and helped her down. Cayenne settled into one of the seats situated on opposite sides of the single outboard and waited as Mel untied the lines.

"You look like you know what to do on these things," Cayenne said.

"I grew up around this." Mel dismissed her, the sound of the engine making conversation difficult, and the boat moved out of the slip. She watched the other boats as they made their way through the marina toward the red and green markers showing the channel to open water. As they passed the last marker, the man pushed down on the throttles and increased speed until the boat came up on plane.

Mel planned her strategy to approach Cayenne as the breeze blew through her short hair. There was no way to talk now as the boat cruised at what she figured was 30 knots. It would take them a little less than an hour to reach the coral farm located in the Sawyer Keys Wildlife Management Area, where Cayenne had somehow obtained a permit to grow the coral.

They headed northwest, quickly covering the five miles to the outside of the barrier made by the myriad of small islands and shoals, which formed a line running fifty miles east to Bahia Honda. Once they passed through a small marked channel that led to deeper water, the man turned northeast. Mel knew from experience that you often had to go backwards before you could go forwards through the intricate waters of the back country. Half an hour later, the boat slowed as they approached a line of buoys one hundred yards off one of the Sawyer Key's mangrove-lined shores.

Mel waited patiently while the man helped Cayenne into her dive gear. As she was about to place her mask on her face and step off the swim platform, she turned. "Too bad you can't come with me. It's really cool."

"Why can't I?" Mel turned to the man. Might as well see what this is all about. "You have any gear? Mask, fins, and a weight belt?"

"Really, you're going to snorkel?" Cayenne asked.

Mel ignored her as she took the fins and mask from the man. "I need about four pounds of weight." She sat on the transom and spit in her mask, rinsed it with water and placed it on her head. The man returned with a weight belt, which she took and placed around her waist before donning the fins. Then she back-rolled off the side of the boat into the water. She surfaced and gave Cayenne a thumbs up.

They both swam on the surface to the first buoy, where Mel watched as Cayenne fumbled for the hose to deflate her BC. She knew the woman lacked experience by the way she swam with her hands. An experienced diver put all their energy into their legs, where the fins could do the work. Without waiting for her, she took several deep breaths to oxygenate her lungs and dove. She finned down, following the line attached to the buoy and observed the small pieces of corral attached to it every few feet.

Just as she reached what felt like twenty feet, Cayenne passed her and she ascended for air. Another few breaths and she inspected the next line.

A few minutes later, both women were on the surface, holding onto the buoy. Cayenne bobbed in the light chop and tried to talk, but kept taking water into her mouth. Mel reached over and inflated her BC for her, allowing the woman's head to clear the surface more easily.

"Wow, you're really good at that. I can barely get down there with all this stuff."

"Just practice. You grow up here, you learn a few things."

"Wish I could do that," Cayenne said as she put her regulator back in her mouth.

Mel looked toward the next buoy, surprised that she was actually enjoying the water. As a teenager, she had been an accomplished free diver. The buoy was only fifty feet away, and she started toward it. She reached the buoy and started her rhythmic breathing sequence, clearing her lungs of CO_2 and filling them with oxygen. After half a dozen breaths, she submerged and followed the line trying to reach the thirty-foot-deep bottom, checking out the horizontal lines attached every few feet, swinging in the current. The starter coral pieces clung to these lines, absorbing nourishment from the passing water.

At twenty feet, she could just make out some structures sitting in the sea grass, but she was out of breath and had to surface. She tried once more to get deeper, but acknowledged her limits—nowhere near the forty feet she had so easily been able to free dive not too many years ago.

They met back on the surface and swam to the boat, Cayenne arriving first. Mel held onto the swim platform while the man helped Cayenne out of the water.

"Did you see anything?" Cayenne asked.

"The coral is pretty cool. I thought I saw something on the bottom but I couldn't get that deep. I guess I'm getting old."

"But what did you see?"

Mel sensed the unease in her voice. "Just some stuff on the bottom. I was a good ten feet away, so it was really hard to tell." She took her fins off, tossed them over the transom, and climbed onto the boat.

"Oh. Those are probably these cool compartments that each piece of coral has to itself. The scientists have this theory that if they're close together, they'll nurture each other and grow faster. We're just starting to experiment with that."

Mel suspected something wasn't right, but was forced to hold her tongue as Cayenne went to the man and whispered something in his ear. He went to the bow and let the line loose, then returned to the helm and started the engines.

They reached the marina an hour later and Cayenne claimed a headache when Mel started to ask questions about finances. She squirmed in her seat as the car worked slowly through the throngs of people. Traffic was heavier now, making the drive longer and even more uncomfortable. Mel quickly left the car and went to her desk to check her email and close up for the day. Before she could leave, Cayenne stormed past her and slammed her office door.

Seconds later, Mel heard her yelling into the phone.

* * *

"What do you mean you took someone out there?" the voice yelled at her.

"I had no idea that girl was like frickin' Jacques Cousteau. She free dives like a fish. I thought she was going to stay on the boat," Cayenne spat back. "And what are you doing putting those things so close to shore? They're in my permit area."

She did not like the man or his attitude, but had been forced into an uneasy yet profitable alliance with him. The Sawyer Keys were a wildlife management area mainly set aside for nesting birds, but the northeast corner had been privately owned before the designation was added. Obtaining a permit to farm coral there had been easy, but the reclusive man that lived on the island was another matter.

He had opposed her project from the beginning, often sabotaging her work. Finally, she had confronted him and made a deal that now looked like it might save her.

"That's the whole point. If they're in the permit area the Feds aren't going to look there. You sure she didn't see anything?" His voice calmed slightly.

"She said she saw some structures in the sea grass, but didn't get to the bottom. Visibility wasn't great. I really doubt it."

"I'm in Miami now, be back in a few days. I'll move them then."

The ceiling fan did little to abate the sweat dripping from her brow as Cayenne looked down at her desk and saw the meager balance on her bank statement. Several other letters were stacked next to her, mostly from the banks that held her loans. The once-healthy trust was almost depleted, and she was getting desperate.

The illegal lobster traps, called casitas, that Jay had placed in the management area held the only cash she was likely to get her hands on.

The word on the docks was that it was a terrible lobster year, and that made prices high. The illegal casitas, placed far from any other traps, were usually filled, and if she could get to the lobster first, it would bring enough cash to keep things afloat for several months. With the call on her line of credit due tomorrow, she had little choice. It was the last of many notices before the bank foreclosed.

"Never mind. I'll take care of it," she said as she twirled her still-damp reddish hair and hung up. Setting aside the bank letter, she reached into her desk drawer and pulled out Mel's resume. Her father had taught her to run a thorough background check on anyone she hired, and she had done that with Mel. The woman had come from DC, and she wasn't sure where her loyalties would lie. There was always the possibility that she worked for her detractors. She knew she had enemies, every non-profit that tried to help the ecosystem did. Some worried that allowing non-profits like hers to exist was a slippery slope towards closing and restricting larger and larger areas of prime fishing and hunting grounds. Others believed these non-profits benefited financially from operating in protected areas. And in this case the latter group was correct.

In the file was a brief about her boyfriend, Mac Travis. She glanced at the summary of salvage and commercial fishing business, and continued reading. Her memory proved accurate when she read the last paragraph about a wayward deckhand of his that had a penchant for trouble.

Chapter 3

Trufante stared at his empty glass, wondering if his credit would handle another one. He looked up at the barmaid and gave his best smile, revealing his thousand-dollar custom grill.

"Hey. I know you want another." The woman smiled back as she looked over her shoulder and took his glass to the tap, where she refilled it. "Just don't tell anyone." She set it down in front of him. "Don't worry. I got it."

Trufante lifted the glass and toasted her. "'Preciate that," he said drawing out the first word with his Cajun accent.

At least there was one bright spot today, he thought, watching her butt sway as she walked away. But his overall state of affairs was troublesome. There were slow seasons in the Keys, but nothing like the drought Mac was now in. Usually the spring months were quiet as lobster and stone crab seasons wound down. The weather was sketchy and there were long spans where they were unable to get offshore for the dolphin fish that were just starting their early summer run. As the weather warmed, though, it was easier to get out.

But this year the fish hadn't been there. Nothing to worry about in the big picture, but right now, it was bad. Ditto for lobster season … at least so far. Lobster would usually hold him into the fall, when stone crab came in season and the snapper and grouper came into the shallow reefs. This year it wasn't happening. He had looked around for other work, but it was the same everywhere. Mac didn't go out every day, like some of the other fishermen, but he paid well and didn't mind if Trufante freelanced.

He was deep into his beer when a long-legged woman pulled out the chair next to him. Turning toward her, he couldn't help but notice her expanded chest.

"Hello there, little lady," he said, putting on his best accent. "Where'd y'all come from?"

"Well hello there, yourself," she said as she slid onto the seat. "Buy you a beer?"

He drained his beer and grinned. Once in a while he could count on getting hit on by a tourist woman, out for a good time with a local. Something romantic about it, he guessed. The barmaid was coming back down the bar and he signaled toward her, allowing the woman to order. A minute later, the drinks were in front of them and she broke the silence.

"I'm Cayenne," she said, holding her hand out.

He took it in his callused palm. "Tru. Really it's Alan Trufante, but my friends call me Tru." He smiled.

They huddled closer as one round became two, and soon the beer was the chaser for the tequila shots they were toasting with.

"You know, I was thinking we maybe could have a time down in Key West," Trufante said as he placed his hand on her knee. He had been more than happy to have her company and let her buy drinks.

"That could be fun," she giggled. "But I was really looking for someone to help me with a little problem I have." She placed her hand over his.

"Thought we were getting on fine. I don't know if we should bugger it up with business."

"Oh, please. We can still have a good time." She slid her hand north.

"Well. What kind of help are you needing?" he asked.

"Just a strong guy and a boat." She squeezed his arm.

19

"Well, I can maybe help with part of that equation, but I don't have a boat."

"Maybe you could borrow one?" she asked as she put her other hand on his other thigh and started walking her fingers up his leg.

He wasn't about to stop her now. This was leading in a very favorable direction. "You want to tell your new friend Tru what exactly you're needing?"

Her hand inched higher. "I got a line on some lobster traps that are abandoned. Heard there might be some money in it. I'd be willing to split it with you."

The alcohol and her boobs pressing against him, never mind the chance for a payday, must have altered his rational thought process. Abandoned traps were often loaded with lobster, and he could sure use the money.

"Maybe we can work something out. I might be needing a little more encouragement, if you get my drift."

She leaned closer. "I've got all the encouragement you need, baby."

* * *

Trufante reluctantly pulled the sheet off and got out of bed. He glanced over at the sleeping body next to him, once again admiring her curves. They might not all be real, but they were fun. Moonlight showed through the thin curtain covering the single window in his room; no sunlight yet.

He thought about waking her, but didn't want her around Mac when he picked up the boat, so he left her where she was. Mac had been fine when he had called last night about taking the boat for service this morning. He hadn't planned on checking his traps for a couple of days, he said. With the season this slow, it was better to save the time and gas money and let the traps soak longer. When things were hot, the commercial limit of 250 lobster per boat per day was easy. You could go out and check half your traps each day and pull those kinds of numbers, but the way this year was going, it took almost three full days of soak and pulling all the pots to limit out.

He left a note on the bathroom vanity with directions to the boat ramp on the Gulf side, where he would pick her up in an hour. Ready to leave, he went back to the bed and patted her butt.

"Wake up, sunshine. I left directions in the bathroom. Meet me in an hour." He made sure she acknowledged him before she closed her eyes again.

Downstairs, he went out to his motorcycle and started the engine, allowing it to warm up for a minute before he climbed on. It was just getting light out when he started down the street. Several turns later he stopped at US1 and waited for the traffic, found a hole, and accelerated into the middle turn lane. He followed the highway for a few miles and turned left onto Mac's street.

"Why don't you stop being an idiot and wear a helmet?" Mac asked as he pulled up.

"Shoot, injures the reputation," he responded.

"Injures your brain is more like it, and I know you don't have insurance." Mac turned away and walked into the house.

"Breakfast." Trufante smelled the bacon as he followed him through the door.

"Mel's upstairs. Go ahead. There's a few things I want to get off the boat before you take it." Mac started to walk through the downstairs workshop. The house, originally built on stilts, as were most houses in the Keys, had the bottom enclosed after the final building inspection, and now housed a small office and large workshop.

Trufante turned and headed up the stairs into the living area. He found Mel deep into her laptop, muttered a quick hello, and went for the stove. After downing several pieces of bacon, he murmured something again and left, thankful that she had been

21

engrossed in whatever her lawyer brain did. Theirs was a mutual-respect relationship, and that was mainly respect by distance. She was critical of Mac for still working with him after all the trouble he found himself in, and which usually involved her and Mac getting him out of.

Back downstairs, he wandered through the workshop looking at the equipment scattered everywhere and walked out the door that led to the water. Mac was taking some fishing rods off the boat and placing them on the dock.

"They said they could fix it while you wait?" Mac asked.

"Sure enough. I told them the windlass has been nothing but trouble since we installed it. I'll hang out—got nothing better to do. You going fishing?"

Mac picked up the rods and walked toward the door, leaning them next to a small cooler. "Yeah, gonna take the paddleboard out and see if I can get into something."

"Well, later then." Trufante turned and walked toward the boat, climbed aboard, and started the engines. Mac came over and slipped the dock lines for him and watched as he pulled forward into the small turning basin at the end of the canal. He slowed, pushed one throttle forward and the other back, and waited while the boat pivoted on its center. Once it was turned, he pushed both throttles to their first stop and idled out of the canal.

The narrow canal opened into a large harbor where he passed several moored sailboats and one wreck from a storm last year. Ten minutes later, he pushed the throttles forward and left the channel, staying parallel to the Seven Mile Bridge. At the fourth opening, he turned hard to starboard and went underneath the new span, crossed a small section of choppy water, and passed under the old span now used as a pedestrian walkway to Pigeon Key. The Gulf opened in front of him and he navigated past a sand bar, its top exposed by the low tide, keeping the single pole that marked it to port. He looked over at the shallow water barely covering the obstacle and turned east.

He passed a few deserted islands and turned to starboard into a cove with a boat ramp and small harbor. There was the usual morning traffic on the ramp and he waited for the dock to clear before pulling the boat up and tying off. He had to admit he was a little surprised when he saw Cayenne waiting, and couldn't help but smile, watching her bounce toward him, almost falling out of her skimpy top. *This might be a good day after all*, he thought as he offered a hand and helped her onto the deck, then grabbed her dive bag and tank.

"You just make yourself comfortable and we'll be right out of here," he said as he coiled and stowed the single dock line he had used to tie off. Back at the helm, he pulled away from the dock. "You might want to give me some direction here."

She came over to him and shaded the screen of her cellphone. "Here. That's where we need to go."

He squinted at the small screen, which showed a pin near an island. "That's a little hard on the eyes. Can you read them numbers off so I can put them in the chart plotter?"

"Numbers?"

"Yeah, the coordinates. You know, the GPS numbers. I'd help you, but my eyes ain't what they used to be."

"OK, Give me a minute and I'll figure it out. I know it's out there." She pointed to the open Gulf.

"Out there's not as easy as it looks. There's more sand bars and shoals than the bayou's got backwater. You're gonna need to be more specific."

She was pecking at the screen with her finger. "I think I have them. One starts with a 1 and the other an 8?"

He nodded and started to enter the numbers in the large screen set into the dashboard. When the last number was entered he pushed the *GOTO* button and the screen changed to a chart, centering on a pin dropped on a cluster of small islands.

"Sawyer Keys? Sound familiar?" he asked.

"That's it. They're right off there." She put her hand around his waist.

"You know there's a sanctuary out there."

"I'm sure they're out of the boundary."

"If you say so." He pushed the throttles forward, the reaction of the boat caused her to grab him tighter, and he smiled to himself as the boat got up on plane and he checked the course. He looked down at the autopilot and thought about taking her down for a quickie, but knew the waters here were too dicey. Smiling at the idea, he decided to postpone it for when they got there.

He set a course north/northwest to get into open water and, once clear of the line of barrier islands, turned west. The ride was easy and soon the GPS beeped, indicating their proximity to the coordinates.

"There's markers here." He pointed at the buoys.

"They're mine. We can tie up there," she said.

"That' asking for trouble," he said.

"Nothing to worry about. No one's out here."

He ignored her and moved closer to the waypoint before setting the boat in neutral. The windlass stalled as he tried to drop the anchor and he went forward to fix it. When he came back, she grabbed his hand and led him below.

Chapter 4

They emerged from the cabin a half-hour later. Cayenne gave him a sheepish smile, then went to her dive bag and started unloading her gear onto the deck. Trufante watched her move as she started assembling the BC and regulator to the tank.

She turned toward him, all business now. "How do we do this?"

"Do what?" he asked. "You've been a little light on the details. I got the part about abandoned traps, but these have buoys. They're marked"

"The buoys are for our coral farm. The traps are a little further out and they're not marked," she smiled. "Promise. The buoys mark lines that are anchored to the bottom. There are short lines every few feet that the coral grows on."

"Coral what?" He looked out at the calm water, wishing his eyes could penetrate the surface. He had an ear for the wrong, and this didn't sound right.

She seemed to sense his mood. "They're loaded. Just tell me what to do."

"Loaded, huh?" He rubbed his forehead and shielded his eyes from the sun as he continued to stare at the water. The lure of the potential payday distracted him and he went toward the starboard side where he released the winch line. The wheel spun slowly as he pulled the steel cable off. "You know how deep it is?"

"I think it's about thirty feet."

He laid the cable on the deck and went for a small buoy with a line attached. "What we're going to have to do is get right on top of them. That means you're going to have to go down and mark the spot with this. Then come back up and we can move the boat."

"We have to move the boat? That's a lot of time and work," she whined.

"Sweetheart, if you want what's in those traps, you've got to pull them straight up. I don't even know if there's enough cable to reach from here."

She looked down. "I'm a little scared to be diving by myself. You're not supposed to do that, you know."

Trufante looked at her. "Ain't nothing to be done about that now. I'll be on the boat. I can see you from here," he said and handed her the buoy.

She shot him a nasty look, tossed her hair back, put the mask over her head, and went to the transom. He grabbed the tank and brought it over to the swim platform where she waited, then helped her into the straps. She was acting like a spoiled teenager, and he hoped they could get this done quickly. The politics of women were *not* in his wheelhouse.

He checked the air and tapped her shoulder, giving a thumbs-up sign. She stood and took a giant stride into the water, submerging awkwardly with the buoy line in hand.

He squinted through the glare trying to follow the bubble trail that marked her progress and location. After several minutes that looked like she was swimming in a circle she surfaced a hundred feet from the boat. He waved her over to the swim platform and helped her on.

"You good for a minute here? Don't worry 'bout the gear. I'll move the boat and you can hook up the trap." Without waiting for a response, he went forward and surveyed the conditions. The marker was close to the boat. If he used the wind and current, he could stay tied up where he was, drift back, and get close enough without moving the boat. He went to the cleat and unhooked the knot, slowly paying line out as the current moved the boat back.

"What are you doing?" she called from the stern.

"Nothing to worry about. Almost got it." He tightened the line in his hands and tied it off. Winch cable in hand, he dragged the hook back toward her. "Now all's you got to do is take this down and hook it up to something in the middle of the trap." He could see her fear through the lens of the foggy mask. "It ain't rocket science. Just hook it up."

Without giving her a chance to respond, he started to throw the cable into the water. Assuming she was correct and the water was thirty feet deep here, fifty feet of cable would allow enough slack.

She took the hook and stood, her entry even less graceful with the steel cable dragging behind. He was almost enjoying her anguish as he sat on the gunwale and waited. Several minutes later she was back, and he used the tank stem to haul her aboard.

"You're being a little rough," she said as she took off her mask and brushed her hair from her face.

"Ain't no charter boat. Let's see how you did." He went forward to the side of the wheel house and started the winch motor. Slowly it picked up the slack in the line, and the motor lowered an octave, the boat jerking. "Got'er now."

The cable was coming in much slower with the weight of the trap. Trufante guided the wire back onto the spool with a gloved hand and leaned over the side of the boat. The trap was visible now, about five feet below the boat. He could see it clearly, and his blood surged. "That's not a trap. That's a casita." There were rules for legal traps, restricting their size, construction and allowing openings for juvenile lobster to escape. Through the water he could see this trap was an illegal trap used by poachers.

"I don't know what you call it, but it's full of lobsters." She stood next to him, watching it come out of the water. The box was about the size of a sheet of plywood with a few hundred compartments, all filled with lobsters. "Wow. We're rich!" she exclaimed.

He scanned the water around them and noticed a few reflections of metal or glass reflecting in the sun, showing the location of other boats. "We ain't rich if we're dead. This is poacher's ground, here. That's why they're not marked." None of the reflections seemed to be moving. "Damage is done now. If anyone was watching, we'd be dead already." He went for the trap. "Hurry up. As long as we got this far, might as well take them." He released a lever and swung the lid open. His jaw dropped as he saw the hundreds of crustaceans glisten in the sun.

Back at the winch he started the motor again. It lifted the casita from the deck and dumped the contents. Without looking at the catch, he swung the trap out of the boat and started to lower the winch line.

"What do I do with them?" she asked.

"Take a broom from the cabin and sweep them in here." He opened a compartment. "Never mind. I'll get that. You need to go back in and release the hook. That thing's too big to do it up here."

Surprised she didn't complain, he watched her gear up and enter the water again while he swept the lobsters into the fish box. A minute later she surfaced.

"Do it again. I got another one."

"Shit, girl. You gotta know you're looking trouble in the eye. Go unhook it, we gotta get out of here." He scanned the water again, thinking that one of the dots on the horizon was getting closer.

"No. You want it unhooked, you go do it."

He turned from the water and looked at her, knowing he was fighting a losing battle. Back at the winch he raised the second trap and quickly had its contents on the deck.

"That's it. We're pushing our luck in a big way." The trap lowered into the water. This time she came back with the hook, and he wound the cable back on the winch, ran forward, and unhooked the line from the mooring buoy, then tossed it over and ran back to the wheelhouse. One of the reflections he had seen earlier had turned into a fairly large boat that he was certain was coming at them. Better to lose a line than get caught. Back at the helm, he fired the engines and pushed the throttles to full, almost knocking Cayenne off her feet.

"What's the bid deal?" she asked as she came over to him and put a hand on the small of his back.

He tried to ignore it and pointed over the port side. "There's the big deal. That ain't no ordinary boat. It looks like the law to me."

"So? We're not doing anything anymore." She slid her hand down to his butt.

He ignored her and started to set course back the way they had come when he saw a small inflatable launch from the larger boat. Decision made, he turned 180 degrees and headed west, skirting the shallows surrounding the island until he turned to port at an unmarked patch of deep water. Johnston Pass led into the shallows of Cudjoe Basin, where he slowed to avoid a shoal.

He turned to check on the pursuit, but they were gone.

Back in deeper water, he got the boat on plane and followed Kemp Channel past the mangrove-lined shores of Cudjoe Key. A bridge was visible in the distance and he zoomed the chart plotter in, trying to get a line on the markers leading through the winding shoals. He slowed the boat as they approached. This was not one of the easier ways into the Atlantic, especially for a large boat, and grounding would be bad.

Once through the pass, he turned and headed east toward Marathon. Several more glances behind him and he relaxed slightly, thinking he had lost his pursuers. The detour had taken them off course, though, and he checked the plotter, which showed them still eighteen miles from Sister Creek, the inlet past Boot Key and near Mac's house. There was no way he was bringing this load into the main harbor and past the gas docks. There was a good chance the marine patrol would be looking for him there. He sat down and wished he had brought a cooler full of beer.

"We OK?" she asked, visibly shaken.

"Ain't sure. I think we lost them through there, but I don't know why they stopped following us. That inflatable could have gone through those waters faster than us."

"Well what do we do now?"

"Now we sell this load and party." He grabbed her butt. "But I'm gonna take the long way in and drop the boat at Mac's. Those boys out there got radios, and the faster we get those tails off the boat the better.

* * *

Mac paddled along the mangroves, dragging a small spoon behind the paddleboard. He had been cruising around hoping for a hit, killing time until the tide change. After a quick check of the sun, he figured it was about three o'clock; the start of the incoming tide. He leaned forward and grabbed the rod from the milk crate he had attached to the deck of the board with bungee cords, and started to reel in the line.

Fishing had been slow so far, but he had enjoyed being on the water by himself. He had paddled through the harbor and turned into the mangrove-lined channel running into Boot Key. Now, with the tide changing, he had to work harder as he moved toward the entrance to Sisters Creek, where the incoming tide often brought big fish with it.

It took a half-hour of paddling for him to reach his spot on the shallows, now flooding with water and baitfish. He reached around and took the small anchor from the cooler tied down behind him and tossed it ahead of the board. The line snapped tight as the hook set, and he waited until he was sure he wasn't moving before he picked up the rod and balanced himself. He aimed for a small outcropping, opened the bail, and cast, allowing the line to free spool after the lure hit the water. The tide took the light line and lure into a small cove. The bail clicked and he started to retrieve the line, jerking every few turns until he felt a tug.

With a quick yank, he pulled the rod to the side to set the hook and checked the drag before he started to reel.

The fish was halfway in when he heard a boat approaching; not unusual here, but he knew the sound of this engine. He kept pressure on the fish as he turned and saw his boat cruise past, faster than the no-wake zone allowed. Suddenly the boat coasted to a stop and he paddled toward it, the rod—secured by his bare foot—still dragging the fish

Trufante leaned over and grabbed his hand as the board coasted up to the swim platform.

"Go ahead and take it." Mac said as he handed up the rod. "And then you can tell me what you're doing blowing through here and not back at the dock. This is a little out of the way from what you said." He saw the flash of red hair and turned to the girl. Typical Trufante he thought.

"I can explain," Trufante said as he pulled the snapper over the transom.

Mac used the dive ladder to enter the boat then hoisted the SUP aboard and slid it to the port side, where he strapped it to the gunwale. He set the paddle down and stared at the couple. "OK. This should be good. Entertain me."

Trufante started to babble some excuse that Mac only half listened to as he watched the water to see if the marine patrol or sheriff had seen Trufante entering the inlet at that speed. They had been together too long for Mac to even wonder how the Cajun got into so much trouble. Usually it was harmless and good for a few laughs or a good ribbing, but once in a while his antics had consequences.

He went to the helm and started to steer toward Boot Key harbor, where he turned and headed for his dock. The boat was turning into the canal when Mac saw several figures standing on the seawall by the dock.

As the boat closed the last hundred yards, he saw that they were in uniform.

Chapter 5

Mac thought about turning the boat and running, but that wasn't going to get him anywhere but deeper into whatever it was that Trufante had gotten him mixed up in this time. If they were on his dock, they knew who he was and what the boat looked like. He looked over at the lanky Cajun as he slowed to approach the dock.

"Spit it out now—and fast," he said.

Trufante started to mumble, and Mac was about to confront him again when he reached over and opened the fish box.

"Oh, man. I don't guess those are from our traps." He looked over at the woman sitting on the opposite gunwale. "She got something to do with this?"

"Shit, it don't matter where we got them. It's not too far over the limit. I'll just tell them I miscounted or something. I can play dumb."

Mac let that one pass with a look. "Well, let's get this settled with the law and then I'll deal with you. Does she at least have a name?"

"Tell him your name, sweetheart," Trufante called over to her.

Cayenne went toward Mac with her hand extended. "Cayenne Cannady. Pleased to meet you."

Mac looked at the figure in front of him—almost falling out of her bathing suit—and wasn't sure what to make of her. "Maybe you can tell me what's going on. Old Tru here seems to have lost his tongue."

Cayenne looked to Trufante for support, but he remained mute. "These were in abandoned traps off my coral farm. The lobster would have just died if we didn't take them."

Mac looked up at the sky in disbelief. If her appearance didn't give it away with her fake boobs, died red hair, and whiter-than-normal smile, she'd just summed it up with the coral farm. He didn't care for politics, not trusting either party, but conservation was important to him. Coral farms were one of those green ideas that looked better on paper than they panned out to be in real life. In many cases, they fronted illegal harvesting. There was no way to tell if a hunk of corral came from a farm or the reef.

"You care to explain that to the *Federales*?" Mac asked her as he coasted up to the dock. Two officers came toward the boat to help with the lines. Once it was tied off, Mac went to disembark.

"Hold on there." One of the men stepped forward, hand on his holster.

"You can take your hand off the gun. No reason for that," Mac said.

"The three of you go stand against the port side there." The officer hopped onto the deck and signaled for one of the other men to watch them. "I need to search this vessel. Who's the captain?"

Mac stepped forward and stopped when the officer nearest to them drew his weapon. "I told you that's not necessary. My name's Mac Travis. It's my boat, and I have a commercial license. I'm guessing you have some kind of just cause or something to come onto my property."

"Holster that weapon, deputy," another man said. "Fish and Game has the authority to search any vessel in our jurisdiction at any time. If you're a commercial fisherman, you ought to know that." He went toward the cabin. "Now let's have a look at your papers."

Mac moved toward the man while the other two officers

boarded the boat. The deck was crowded now, as the men started their search. He went into the cabin and opened the chart table with one eye on the deck.

"Here." He grabbed a stack of papers and handed them to the officer. "Permits, registration, it's all there and current." Telling the truth, or at least what he knew of it, was probably the easiest way out of this. He knew he was in trouble, and probably big trouble. The least he could face was a fine, that he would of course have to front that for Trufante who was always broke, The worst was the loss of his commercial license and maybe his boat, which would put him out of work. Add that to the loss of the cache on the reef and things were looking bad. How he handled this could be the difference. "I'll tell you right now that my mate there—" He pointed to Trufante. "—Took that woman out, and they're over the limit. Lobsters are in there." He motioned to the fish box just before the deputy lifted the lid.

They left the cabin and joined the gathering of people staring into the fish box filled with lobster. "Go ahead and start with these. You know the drill; check the size and get a count," the officer said. He looked up at another deputy. "And keep looking." Then he turned to Mac. "What're you doing aboard if you weren't with them?"

Mac pointed to the paddleboard. "I was out fishing when they cruised past. Just got a ride back, is all."

"Hate to break it to you, but it's your license and your vessel. Doesn't matter who's on board and who's not," the officer said.

Mac looked at Trufante and shook his head, wondering how bad this was going to get. He sat down on the gunwale and watched as the lobsters were pulled one at a time from the fish box. They were stacked in two piles; one of legal size, the other with shorts. He was starting to calculate the fine in his head when the head man came over to him.

"Mr. Travis, my boss is coming over here with some papers and some bad news for you. I'm going to do you a favor and tell you what we know and let you call a lawyer, if you want."

Mac nodded.

"We had a boat out by the Sawyer Keys pulling casitas. It's pretty high on our priorities to eradicate all those illegal habitats out there."

Casitas, Mac thought. *That's what this is about.* He had seen a chart in the Deptartment of Fish and Game newsletter showing how the the illegal traps were heavily concentrated in that area. That had to be how Trufante had gotten this many lobster.

The man continued, "This boat was working an area we were about to hit, so we sent an inflatable out to see what was going on. Your man here pulled out before we could get there and hightailed it through the backcountry. We have orders not to pursue out of sight of the base boat, so the inflatable didn't follow."

Mac looked over at Trufante again. He didn't look worried at all, sitting there playing grab ass with the redhead. "You hear what he's saying, Tru?"

Trufante looked up. "Yeah. That's about it. Sorry, Mac."

"In a marine sanctuary on top of it. Now the feds are involved."

"Sorry," Trufante muttered again.

"Sorry." He was at a loss for words. This could cost him his boat. NOAA was becoming increasingly involved in both the removal of the casitas and the prosecution of those involved. The federal agency started using the laws of civil forfeiture to confiscate property in these cases. As the chart in the newsletter had shown, the largest concentration of casitas were in and around marine sanctuaries. He and the other commercial fishermen steered clear of the protected areas and he knew there was a good probability that a NOAA boat had been working the Sawyers Keys area when Trufante was there. He turned to the officer. "I don't have my phone on me. Can I go in the house and make a call?"

"You're good until my boss gets here," the man said, and turned his attention to the lobster crawling around the deck.

Mac jumped onto the dock and strode to the house. He went up the back stairs, opened the sliding glass door to his bedroom, and made his way to the kitchen, where he yanked the phone from its charging cord and checked the screen for messages. It was blank.

He opened the phone app and hit Mel's number. Pacing the room while the phone rang, he wondered how she was going to take this.

She answered on the fourth ring. "Where are you?" he asked.

"I'm fine thanks, how are you?"

"Sorry. I got trouble here at the house. Fish and Game and some suits. Trufante took the boat ..."

She cut him off, her tone changing entirely. "Stall them for ten minutes. I'm just getting off the Seven Mile Bridge. Don't say anything to anyone and keep that stupid Cajun quiet."

Mac put the phone in his pocket, pulled the charger from the wall, and went back to the bedroom. Mel was good—very good—but this kind of law was a little out of her wheelhouse. He feared what was about to happen. Casitas were the bane of legitimate lobster men. Instead of the approved traps, which allowed undersized lobsters to escape, these unmarked and illegal devices could hold hundreds of lobster in one spot, without regard to size.

They were the tools of poachers, and known to be out of bounds.

There had been several cases lately where offenders accused of poaching had lost their boats, houses, and vehicles. Most fishermen didn't have the capital or concern to set up a corporation to protect themselves and their assets, so if the law came after them, that was the end. After deciding he had everything he needed, he went downstairs through the workshop and into the office. From the desk he grabbed a handheld GPS, then went to the safe and unlocked it.

He heard someone try the rollup door and quickly grabbed the felt bag with the last of his gold and a thumb drive and shoved them in his pocket. The safe closed, he turned to see two men and a woman standing in the doorway. One was the officer from the boat; the other was dressed in a suit, his brow sweating, clearly uncomfortable in the humidity.

"We'll take the GPS. Could be evidence on there," One of the men said.

Mac handed him the unit and turned to the woman—the local sheriff, whom he knew well. "Jules, can you tell me what's going on here?"

"I heard some stuff on the radio and figured I'd come and see if I could buffer this a little. It's got nothing to do with the sheriff's office, but I'm here to vouch for you, or do whatever I can," she said, her tone somber.

Before he could thank her, the man in the suit handed him a stack of documents. "I'm Bill Harris, district attorney for Monroe County, and I'm here to personally serve these papers and confiscate the property indicated."

This was happening way too fast. Mac took the papers and scanned them. One named his boat and the other the house. They were charging him with poaching in the marine sanctuary and trying to take everything he had. He tried to hide his anxiety and took his time reading them, hoping that Mel would barge in at any second and help him.

"Jules," he looked up. "Can't you help with this?" He hoped his long time friend could help him out.

"Sorry, Mac. I checked that they dotted their I's and crossed their T's, but that's all I can do."

The group turned as the front door opened and Mel burst through.

"Jules, thank God. Can you tell me what these idiots are into now?" She went to Mac and grabbed the papers from his hand, leaned against the desk, and started reading.

"You better hear it from them. I'm just here to give some moral support and make sure they follow procedure. If they're going to arrest him, I can try and take him in here and get bail set. Otherwise they might take him to Miami and put him in a Federal prison. It'll be a lot harder to get him out then."

She looked up from the papers. "It's the boat and the house, Mac. Casitas, really. I'd figure Tru for that, but not you."

Mac looked at her. "I have nothing to do with this. There's some redheaded bimbo out there that suckered Trufante into this."

She didn't wait to hear more, and stormed out of the room, heading for the open back door and the dock. Mac followed the group outside wondering how this was going to play out. But, before she reached the dock she stopped and was about to turn towards the lead agent but did a double take and stared at the boat for a long second before facing the agent.

"So this happens now?"

"Yes, ma'am, I have the authority to take the boat and lock the house. Both items will be held. If he's found guilty, they will be auctioned off."

From the way the conversation was going, Mac figured there was nothing she could do … at least now. If there had even been a tiny crack in the legal veneer or paperwork she would have pried it apart.

"It is what it is. I think she'll have to take you three into custody." He looked at Jules.

"He's right, Mac. I have a car on the way for those two on the boat." She looked toward the dock. "You can ride with me. I'll make sure you can get bail tonight."

He looked at Mel hoping she would have his back.

"Yeah, I won't leave you hanging. Let me just grab a few things before they lock us out," she said.

He looked after her as she headed upstairs.

Mac stood helpless his fingers deep in his pockets, protecting his last assets. The small amount of gold would not get him far, but the information on the thumb drive might.

Chapter 6

Mel stared at the ceiling, exhausted, trying to count the dots on the acoustic tiles. She had run out of things to do or even think about an hour ago. It was close to nine, according to the clock on the wall, and she had been waiting for hours. The first few hours had been hectic; nonstop phone work to try and make a deal. First she had pulled some strings to keep Mac in Marathon with the local authorities, instead of him being transported to Miami and held in Federal prison. Then she had negotiated his release and obtained a bail bond. Not the kind of work she was used to doing, but she had called in several favors and finally gotten it done. Jules had come out and reassured her a while ago that things were moving forward and Mac should be released soon.

The time had given her an opportunity to think and plan. She had seen the red-head on the boat, her boss, Cayenne. She had to be behind this and Trufante was a pawn in her game. She believed Mac was innocent. The challenge was that it was his boat. The Feds had already confiscated the boat and moved it to a marina on the Gulf side. The house was an even larger issue. The court order allowed the house to be locked as a crime scene and if Mac was indicted, and proven guilty, it could be auctioned under the civil forfeiture act.

She had little time to fight to save both assets, and needed an immediate solution—like where to sleep tonight. The battery on her phone had gone dead, so she had nothing to do but think and count little dots on the ceiling.

Her thoughts were troubling. Yes, she loved Mac, but there was seldom a lull in his adventures ... or, better stated, the misadventures of Alan Trufante, which Mac always got tangled up in. Sooner or later—and with Trufante's luck it would be sooner—something really bad was going to happen. And this might be it. Without the boat, Mac had no way to make money. With that and the loss of his cache on the reef, she suspected he was near broke. If he lost the boat and the house, he would have to start from scratch.

She was less worried about herself; with a law degree and her experience, she could find work. There was always opportunity in DC. Her count was interrupted—just as she started to think about Cayenne and her involvement—by the door opening.

Mac walked out, head held low, and she immediately got out of the chair and went to him. Together they walked out of the building and to the truck. They got in and Mel pulled out of the parking lot and onto US1.

"Where do we go?"

"Mel," he stuttered. "I'm so sorry about all this."

She punched his arm. "I know it was the lame-brain Cajun. The only thing I'm mad about is that you still hang out with him. Why'd you let him take the boat?" She figured berating him would serve no purpose now.

"He was supposed to go get the windlass fixed. Broke it last week and it was his fault. I didn't see any harm in that until I saw him flying through Sisters Creek with that redheaded bimbo. It's really hard to find help here."

"That redheaded bimbo, huh?" Mel said as they pulled into a strip center parking lot with a barbecue restaurant on the end.

Mac got out of the truck and went to the door. He held it open for Mel to enter and the conversation was put on hold as they ordered food and sat down.

"We need a plan." Mel said. "They impounded the boat and locked up the house."

"I don't know. Maybe the best thing for me is to go out to your dad's place and figure this out. Humanity is rubbing me the wrong way right about now." He noticed her look. "I was talking about *us* going out there," he corrected himself.

Her look remained unchanged. "That's not what I was thinking about. I know you have no issue running from your problems, but this needs to be handled, and quickly. The faster we can figure this out, the better chance you have of walking away unscathed."

Their food came and they started to eat.

"What do you mean figure this out?" Mac asked as he set a stripped rib bone down and wiped his hands.

Mel took a bite of her sandwich, "The Feds are not going to solve this. The burden is on you to prove that you're innocent. They think they've already done their job catching you and confiscating your property. There's probably some high-level backslapping going on right now at your expense." She stopped and finished eating.

"Here's what I've been thinking about. You want to find a boat and go out to my dad's for a while, and that could work. I ought to give you a bunch of crap about running away, but I'll save that. From his place, you can scout out the area and see who *owns* those casitas. Find out what's really been going on out there."

"And it doesn't sound like you're coming with me."

She looked at him with as much empathy as she could. "Mac, I can help more from Key West. The legal system is my tool." She finished the last french fry and pushed her plate away. "What about a boat? How are you going to get out there?"

"I can take a board and paddle out. Your dad's skiff is still there, and I've been meaning to have a look at that boat that's wrecked on the beach."

"Figured you had a plan. You good if I take the truck?"

"Better you than the Feds."

STEVEN BECKER

* * *

Mac watched as Mel pulled out of the driveway and waved to him. He walked to the front door and tugged on the lock placed there by the authorities. A bright yellow notice stated that the house had been confiscated and could be auctioned at a to-be-announced date. He felt like tearing it off, but thought better of it. Around the side of the house, he found the neglected kayak leaning against the stucco and pushed it over. It was an old sit-on-top, and hadn't been used in several years, since he had discovered paddleboards. But his best board had been on the boat when the Feds took it, and if he were going to make the passage to Wood's Island at night, the kayak was the safer vessel.

Spiders crawled frantically from the shell as he pulled it to the seawall and went back for the paddle and his backpack. The night was dark and he knew the moon, though it would be near full, wouldn't rise for several hours. An unlit boat at night was dangerous and illegal. A light would be essential for the trip, especially as he had to pass under the Seven Mile Bridge on his way to the Gulf side. Even at this time of night, there would be anglers and boat traffic. Without a light, the kayak sitting low in the water would be invisible to passing traffic.

He walked around the house, looking for anything that could illuminate the kayak enough to warn boaters, but found nothing. About to give up, he dug in his pocket and retrieved his phone. It would wear down the battery—if it even made it the entire three hours he expected the paddle would take—but the camera flash would put off enough light. The problem now was keeping it dry. The motion sensor detected his movement and he looked up at the lights on the back porch, which came on when he walked past. Each light was surrounded by a glass globe in the shape of a jelly jar. If he could seal the bottom, the globe would protect the phone. He climbed the stairs and retrieved one, juggling the hot glass from hand to hand as he descended.

42

He dragged the kayak to the edge of the seawall, then took the phone and placed it inside the globe and started looking for a way to seal the open end. The plastic kayak had several drink holders molded into it and he stuck the globe into one. Happy with the fit, he placed the phone in the jar, reset it in the holder, and dragged the boat to the edge of the seawall.

He needed to get out of there quickly, before someone reported seeing him, and the light was a sure giveaway. So he pushed the front end of the boat over the wall and into the water four feet below. Careful not to lose control, he leaned down and then got on his belly with his arms extended to the water to place the stern in. The kayak bobbed in the light chop as he eased his body over the seawall, using the wall to brace the unstable craft until he could sit.

He started paddling out of the canal and toward Boot Harbor. The sensation of paddling at night was unique. All his senses were on full alert, looking for obstacles in the ink black water ahead. Twenty minutes later, he was warmed up and heading out the Knight's Key channel. As soon as he passed the second marker, he cut to starboard across the shallow bottom. He never would have tried that maneuver in a power boat, but with high tide and the negligible draft of the kayak, he sailed across the flats, spooking several fish that jumped in front of him.

The Seven Mile Bridge lay ahead of him now and he took a few deep breaths, knowing what was coming. The current through the spans was noticeable even in a power boat. If he faltered for any reason, he would be pushed back or—worse—slammed into one of the piers. Ready, he put his head down and paddled hard, remembering advice he had heard somewhere—"*Whatever happens, paddle harder*".

Five minutes later he was catching his breath on the calmer Gulf side.

The crux of the trip over, he settled into an easy rhythm as he paddled the five miles to Wood's Island. The paddle was uneventful, the light from his phone bright enough to alert the few boats that passed that he was there. He figured it was two hours later when the boat kissed the small, sandy beach. His legs were shaky for the first few steps, but he quickly recovered and hauled the boat up the beach to a clump of mangroves that were pulled aside to reveal a clearing with a small skiff on a trailer.

Usually the mangrove branches *hid* the clearing, and he was sure he had left it that way the last time he was here.

He slid the kayak next to the other boat, yanked the jar from the cup holder, and used the now-dim light from the phone to replace the mangroves. The trail was overgrown from lack of use and the mosquitos found him, but he held the light in front of him and pushed through the brush until the trail ended at a clearing with a small stilt house and shed.

* * *

Cayenne squinted as the group walked through the doors of the sheriff's station and out to the sun-baked parking lot. Two attorneys flanked her and a confused Trufante followed. The sweat and salt from yesterday still coated her skin, and she worried her hair was a shade darker from the dirty jail cell. She waited until they were in the rented sedan and the air conditioner was blasting before she spoke.

"Where can we drop you?" She looked at Trufante and drank from a water bottle one of the suits handed her.

"I want to thank y'all for springin' me. Don't know when Mac would've got around to it."

"Please answer the question," Cayenne continued. "I want to be clear here. You are to forget ever seeing me. You don't remember what I look like, what color my hair is, or the size of my chest. You got that?"

"Well, shit. I thought we were gettin' on fine."

She sighed. "You don't get it, do you?" The best way to buy

his silence was to get him out of jail and defend him. Left in there, the Feds would make a deal or interrogate him.

And that would not work in her favor.

Her lawyers had pleaded her absolute innocence, claiming she had just gone for a boat ride. But she needed this guy to go along with it if she were going to maintain that as her story.

"How about this? If you play your part, I can send one of these nice men to defend you at your trial. Probation guaranteed. Otherwise, I can run back in there and file a restraining order against you and rescind your bail."

"I might be slow, but I'm gettin' your drift. My bike is at Mac's. You can drop me there." He leaned back.

They pulled into Mac's driveway ten minutes of silence later and dropped the Cajun in the driveway. Without a word, Cayenne turned away from him and waited to be driven home.

Chapter 7

Mel ran along the beach barefoot, letting the feel of the hard, wet sand by the tide line burn off her anger. She had slept little, turning the puzzle around in her mind, but the pieces still didn't fit. The sun was only three-quarters above the horizon as she picked up the pace for the last stretch of beach, hoping it would clear her head. She arrived, out of breath, at the public restrooms located at the end of Duval Street, and found her running shoes where she had stashed them earlier. Thankfully it was too early for the homeless people in the area to be on the prowl. The stopwatch on her phone showed she had run for almost forty minutes; not a bad time for five miles, especially with two of them in the sand. She felt better, but was no closer to an answer.

There was no one around as she stuck her phone into her shoe and headed back to the water. When she was waist deep, she pivoted and submerged herself, emerging in a breast stroke. She swam into the waves until she was out of breath, then turned and stroked in, using the lights on the restroom to guide her.

The sun, just over the horizon, started to dry her and she retrieved her shoes. She sat on a bench and checked her phone again, hoping for a message from Mac, before replacing it in her armband and putting her shoes back on. Still nothing from him; not all that unusual, but a quick text would have been nice, especially after she had bailed him out.

She slowed her pace on the return trip to the house that served as both Cayenne's residence and the Coral Garden's headquarters. Ten minutes later she had covered the mile to the house and slowed to a walk. She turned to the driveway before entering and noticed that Cayenne's Prius was still not there.

Inside, she checked her email and went to shower. She started thinking about Mac as the water ran over her. Their relationship went back to her high school years, longer ago than her almost forty years wanted to admit. Her dad, an engineering contractor and salvager, had hired Mac out of desperation to repair a bridge, and they had been inseparable for the next twenty years.

Until her father had died.

It still irked her that the two held secrets that she wasn't privy to, but she had gone through a rebellious period in her twenties and gone *"off the reservation"*, as her father said. All she wanted as a teenager was to get out of the Keys, and after graduation she had gone to college and then law school at Virginia. With her connections from several summers working as an intern in DC, she landed a position with the ACLU after graduation— something her conservative father had never forgiven her for.

As she had aged, her views changed, and she realized that you couldn't legislate utopia. Even worse, if you followed the money that paid for the ACLU's suits, it often led where you didn't want to go. She'd left the liberal den of the ACLU and moved in with Mac several years ago. Infatuated with him as a teenager, she knew now that the seven-year age difference was too much when she was seventeen and he was twenty-four, but had a whole different ring to it when you said thirty-nine and forty-six.

It had taken years to get over the teenage crush, and there had been some rough patches in their friendship, some the result of her career choice—he always seemed to back her father and others, with the bad relationships he found himself in … or, as she saw it, was trapped in. With the exception of the last two years, they had hardly spoken for a decade.

She turned the water off, toweled herself dry, and started to think about yesterday. As she dressed, she reviewed what she knew. There wasn't a chance that Mac was a poacher. That much she was sure of. At her desk now, she checked her email again and pulled out a legal pad and pen. There was nothing important in her inbox, and she looked away from the screen and stared at the blank page, finally writing a name in the middle of the paper. She circled it and started stabbing the page with her pen, hoping it would work like a voodoo doll; somehow all roads led to Cayenne Cannady.

* * *

Mac didn't have an agenda and lazed around the upstairs living quarters of the small stilt house until the heat forced him outside. He went to turn the fan on, and remembered the power was out. When he'd come in the night before, the lights hadn't worked, and he'd figured the solar system had shorted in a storm— a fairly common occurrence in the summer. The room heated quickly as the windows were still boarded up; the single open door providing little ventilation. He went outside to the covered porch and down the stairs of the house, crossed the clearing, and walked over to the small shed.

Then something caught his eye as he went to unlock the door. The lock looked like it had been hammered, and now he remembered the mangrove branches that concealed the boats being out of place when he arrived. Someone had been out here.

Circling the building, he saw a blank spot on the wall with bare wires sticking from several conduits, where the inverter for the solar system had been. That explained why there was no power. He went back to the door knob and inserted the key, hoping the lock was not damaged. Wood had constructed the buildings here to withstand hurricanes, and without access through the door he would have to tear half the windowless building apart to get in.

The key turned in the lock and he breathed a sigh of relief as the door opened. The inside was just as he had left it: Batteries for the solar system were stacked in racks against one wall, and a workbench sat on several drawers full of tools across from it. The far wall was covered with diving and fishing gear. He grabbed a cordless drill, hoping the battery was charged enough to remove the screws from the plywood protecting the windows, and went back to the house.

The solar system was a setback; the missing inverter converted the 12 volts supplied by the photo-voltaic panels to the 110 volts needed for some of the tools and equipment. But he figured he could wire the panels directly to the battery bank to turn on the 12-volt lights and pumps, at least.

The house cooled as soon as the plywood was removed and the windows opened. Wood had used a passive solar design when he built the house, situating the windows to the southeast to take advantage of the prevalent direction of the winds here. The thatch roof, constructed from palm fronds, had two ventilation rings near its apex, allowing convection to suck the hot air out through the roof, while bringing cooler air in through the windows. The large overhangs and covered porch worked to shade the interior from the hot afternoon sun.

His next thought was for his rumbling stomach. Back outside, he checked the chest freezer below the house and quickly closed the lid. The freezer was one of the appliances that ran on 110 volts and from the smell, it hadn't been running for a while. He went to the hand pump, filled a bucket with water, and headed upstairs. Until he rewired the solar system, there would be no running water. The refrigerator in the small kitchen ran on propane though and still worked. A few beers and some butter were the sole occupants of the cooler section, but in the small freezer compartment he found two lobster tails. He laid these on the counter and went outside.

While the tails thawed, he went back to the shed, figuring the solar system should be his next priority. The batteries and charge controller checked out, and he took a spool of wire, some cutters, and wire nuts back outside with him. In theory, he only needed to connect the hanging wires together and the system would work; but without a means of disconnect in between, he would have to make the connections hot. He quickly made five of the six connections and then picked up a pair of lineman's pliers to connect the wires. With one hand he grasped the insulated wires, and with the other used the flat-jawed pliers to twist the bare copper together. He flinched when the wires touched and sparked. Once they were connected, he took a large wire nut and threaded it over the joint.

Back inside, he checked the charge controller, now buzzing as the voltage from the solar panels on the roof surged through it. Green lights were illuminated on the display, showing that the unit was functioning. He wiped his brow and relaxed. Now for some food.

He went back upstairs and into the house to check on the lobster tails—now mostly thawed—and took them down to the gas grill under the house. Fifteen minutes later he was relaxing upstairs, the fan spinning mindlessly above him, a plate of lobster and a cold beer from the refrigerator on the table.

As content as he was, he knew he had to make a plan. Once he finished with his lunch he set the plate in the sink and went back outside to the shed. He pulled a variety of fishing gear from the back wall, put it outside, and started organizing it. Next he took a small gas can and a machete and headed back toward the beach.

As he approached Wood's old skiff, he realized that it was improbable that the only thing stolen was the inverter. The island had been uninhabited for almost two years. He had come out and checked it once every month or so, but with the exception of a brief stay by Mel last year, it looked abandoned. Thieves would have taken anything they could have gotten their hands on. The aluminum hull was undamaged, but the motor was gone. Now his situation was looking grim. He could use the kayak to fish and check traps, but he couldn't cover anywhere near the area the motor boat could—and successful fishing was all about covering ground. But he knew he needed a boat with a motor to scout the area Trufante and the woman had been poaching.

Using the machete, he slashed at the palm fronds and mangrove branches encroaching on the trail, and arrived back at the clearing covered in sweat. He was tense and nervous, and the labor of clearing the trail had done little to take the edge off. It was a strange feeling having things stolen from you, but unless you lived here you had to expect it. Since Wood had died no one had set foot out here for months at a time. The house and shed were burglar proof, but as he had witnessed, the inverter and motor had proven to be fair game.

Tired and hungry, he went for his phone to see how Mel was. Though it was far from the first time he had thought of her today, he rarely communicated with her ... or anyone, unless he needed something. The power was off on his phone, and he pushed the button on top.

Nothing happened.

The battery must have drained from using the light last night. He hadn't worried about that, as he'd assumed he could just plug it in to recharge, but without 110-volt power that was impossible. He searched the drawers and cabinets for anything with a cigarette lighter attachment that he could rig to charge it with the 12 volts available, but came up empty handed.

Chapter 8

Sometime during the night, the wind and rain woke him from a sound sleep. He got up and closed the windows, and then he moved from the couch where he had fallen asleep to the bedroom. It was a little after four and he lay in bed, unable to sleep. The wind was not the culprit; it was the first time since leaving his house that he had taken enough time to think about his situation.

Up until now, he had been focused on getting out of town and basic survival. Although he didn't have the food stores to last long, with the fertile waters in his backyard, he knew he could find food. Wood had set the house up to collect fresh water using two five-hundred-gallon tanks to collect the rain runoff from the roof. A 12-volt pump pushed water to a black tank on the roof, where it was heated by the sun. That provided enough hot water for at least a day. Most of the year, when it often rained at least once a day, the tanks remained full. And using fifty gallons a day meant that there were almost three weeks' worth of water to hold through the dry season, when it rained less frequently. As far as he knew, the tanks had never run dry.

Knowing his basic needs were met, he started to toss and turn, trying to figure out how to clear his name and get his boat and house back. As far as he was concerned, Trufante could go down with the ship. He knew Mel could only defend him to a point. She had been instrumental in getting him released quickly, but he knew how emotional she could get about her causes and her work, and that would get in the way at some point. This was too close to home for her to stay objective. As Mel had said, the burden was on him to clear his name.

With his stash on the reef gone, he had no assets to hire a lawyer … and he suspected he would need a good one to get out of this mess. The red-haired woman with the fake boobs held the key. He was sure of it. Trufante wasn't motivated or shrewd enough to think up and execute something like this on his own. Those casitas had been down there before him, and the woman knew exactly where they were. Which meant she was the one at fault here. And she'd pulled Trufante into the mess.

The sun was starting to rise now and he did what he was best at and put his problems on the back burner. He went outside to get some water and noticed the sway of the trees. His plan had been to take the kayak out to catch some fish and then check some unmarked lobster traps that Wood had on a nearby reef. But with the wind blowing what he figured to be 15 knots, the kayak would be unmanageable. For now, he was stranded and out of food.

Back upstairs, he turned on the 12-volt marine radio and tuned to the weather station. The forecast was not favorable for the next day or so. Fifteen to twenty-knot winds were expected today, tonight, and into tomorrow. He thought about the skiff sitting without a motor, but realized that without power that was worse than the kayak. There was a wrecked boat on the other side of the island that was worth a look.

He drank a large glass of water to fill his empty stomach and cursed himself for taking the food staples off the island to control the rat population. But there was still a chance he could catch some fish on the better-protected north side of the island while he checked out the wreck. The sand flats there extended out quite a ways, but he could wade out to deeper water and try and cast to a hole or depression that might hold fish. Considering the weather, it was his best chance for food, and with no other plan, he gathered the gear he had set by the shed, grabbed the machete, and set out on the little-used path, slashing at the growth as he went.

Soon the tangle of branches opened to a small beach overlooking a shallow lagoon protected from the wind. The light green water extended for several hundred yards before it turned slightly darker. If there were any fish they would be in the darker, deeper water. He cut a sturdy branch about four feet long and skinned the wet bark from it. Using it as a wading staff, he grabbed a fishing rod, stuck a box with several lures in his pocket, and started wading toward the deeper water, shuffling his feet as he went to scare off any stingrays in his path.

The tide pulled at his ankles as he reached the color change and stuck the pole in the sand. For several minutes he stood there observing the water, looking for any clues that would lead him to fish. Most fishermen made the mistake of walking up to a piece of water and blindly tossing a line in. Taking the time to read the water was often the difference between success and failure. Even the smallest structure could hold fish, and he soon spotted several birds diving on an area of disturbed water. Without taking his eye off the spot, he unhooked the lure from the eye on the rod, released a few feet of line, and cast. The lure hit about ten feet past the swirling water, as he intended, and he started reeling, jerking the rod as the lure closed in on the action. As it reached the area he gave a quick pull and the rod bent over.

All his problems were forgotten as he focused on the jumping fish. It was too far away to see, but he hoped it was edible. Bonefish and permit patrolled these flats, and on many days he would be delighted to hook one, but neither fish were good table fare. After several runs, each shorter in intensity and duration, he turned the fish and started taking in line as it came toward him. Now he needed to land it, but he had neglected to bring a net or gaff out with him. Dragging the fish to the shore was an option, but he dismissed it as being too risky, as the hook could easily slip from the fish's mouth.

When you were fishing for tonight's dinner, you tended to be more careful.

As it came toward him, he set the rod between his knees and leaned over to scoop the fish out of the water. The twenty-four-inch sea trout was slimy, and escaped his grasp on his first attempt, but he wiped his hands on his cargo shorts and bent over for another try. This time he was able to grab the fish and held it tightly as it started flapping as soon as it left the water.

Finally it quieted down, and he stuck his index finger through its gills and used his thumb to secure it. With the other hand he took the fishing pole, its line still hooked to the fish in case something happened on the way in, and put it under his arm. He pulled the branch from the sand and started to wade for shore.

Still smiling, he reached the shallow water of the flat, where he saw the small white spot showing the location of the boat through the mangroves crowding the edge of the beach. A little surprised that it was still there after two years, especially as close to the waterline as he remembered, he grinned again. He knew the boat was probably in bad shape, but still worth a look. It brought back some bad memories, though, and the smile left his face as he remembered how the man driving the boat had been spying on him and Wood, but hadn't known the water around the small island and had run aground, severely wounding his friend in the process.

The incident had started a chain reaction that led to Wood's death while stopping a terrorist plot.

He reached the beach, set his gear and the fish down, and went to a small palm tree, where he pulled a leaf off. With the fish ensconced in the palm leaf, he buried it in the sand to keep the birds away and headed toward the end of the beach. He had to wade to get around the mangroves, but soon found himself in a small clearing, the surrounding brush making the wreck almost invisible from the water.

The boat lay as he remembered it, the blood stains erased by time and weather. Mosquitos swarmed as he leaned over the gunwale and noticed the two feet of water in the cockpit. He moved toward the bow and saw the large hole right on the water line, where the man had hit the sandbar in the shallows, launching the boat toward its resting place. Moving around the boat, he checked the outboard engine—still attached to the twenty-two-foot hull. The bracket must have broken, allowing the motor to hinge when it hit, possibly saving the engine.

There weren't many engines that he *couldn't* get to start, so he went back to look at the damage to the hull. Mosquitos instantly attacked him as he bent over to examine it, and he pulled his head back, swatting at the critters. He went back to the transom and dug a small hole in the sand, reached in, and unscrewed the plug. That would remove the water and hopefully scatter the pests.

Water was soon flowing out onto the sand. Without a pump it would take at least an hour to drain the hull, though, so he decided to go back to the house, clean the fish, and come back later with some tools.

If things went right, this could be the answer to his problems.

* * *

Cayenne cursed under her breath when she pulled up and saw the truck in the driveway. She had hoped to find the house empty after yesterday's fiasco. What was Mel doing here, while her boyfriend was in the process of losing everything he owned? Surely she had better things to do than tell her how bad a business woman she was.

It really was about time to let her go, she realized.

She ran her hands through her oily hair, desperately in need of conditioner, and tried to look presentable enough to get past the gatekeeper and into her inner sanctum. She was sure that Mel hadn't seen her on the boat yesterday, and also confident that Mac—though her boyfriend—didn't know who Cayenne herself was. If she could get past her, she could lock herself in her room, recover from her night in jail, and figure out what to do next. Eventually she would face Mel, and see if she was suspicious.

She entered and called out for Mel, hoping she was not at her desk. If she was, there would be no way to reach the privacy of her bedroom without passing her.

"Over here," came Mel's voice.

Cayenne cursed again. "Hey. I got some stuff in the car. Can you give me a hand?" she said as she turned into a small room off the kitchen and hid.

"Sure."

Mel walked past her and out the door. Cayenne didn't hesitate, using the ruse to run to her bedroom and lock the door. Relieved she had made it past the other woman without being seen, she quickly stripped off the sundress and bathing suit she had been wearing since yesterday and went for the shower. She washed everything twice and shaved her legs, just to make sure nothing clung to her from the prison cell.

Satisfied that she was free from infectious disease and feeling better, she toweled off and went to bed. She lay there unmoving, trying to figure out what her exposure was.

She had spent the most time with Trufante, but she was sure he had no clue to her identity. The only thing he might recognize were her boobs, which he had stared at obsessively. As for Mel's boyfriend, he was more interested in the lobsters than her. The police had kept them separate in jail and although she had heard Mel, she didn't think she had been seen.. It seemed like she was in the clear. Her lawyers would handle the details, if there were any. She had pleaded the innocent bystander, just taken for a boat ride and as far as she knew, there were no charges pending against her.

The casitas were more of a problem. The Feds knew the approximate if not exact location now, and they would soon figure out that they were in her permit area. She probably had another day to deal with that, she thought, as there had been whitecaps on the water when they drove back from Marathon. You didn't have to be around the Keys very long to know that when the water looked like that, no one went out. She just needed to get the traps removed before the wind died down and the authorities went to have a look.

She reached in her purse for her cell phone, scrolled through the contacts, and pressed one. A man answered after the second ring.

"Sweetheart. So nice of you to call. Do you miss me?"

It took all she had to control her temper and she thought she might need another shower after she finished the call. "Don't you 'sweetheart' me. Are you back?"

"Why? Do you want me to stop by?" he asked.

Again she tried to calm down. Jay was best handled with a delicate touch when you needed something from him. Losing her temper was not going to help anything. "Well, maybe the girls are lonely. But first I need you to get rid of those casitas by the farm. I don't want to get into it now, but I expect the Feds to be crawling all over that place as soon as the wind dies."

"Sweetheart, your wish is my command. That spot's about played out, anyway. Now when do I get to see those beauties?"

Chapter 9

The water had drained and, with the exception of a few stragglers, the mosquitos had scattered by the time Mac returned with the last load of supplies. After a lunch of grilled fish, it had taken him several trips to bring over the materials and tools he needed to start work on the boat. His first task was to free the hull from the suction of the sand and inspect the bottom for damage. There was likely work needed there, as well, and he wanted to know the scope of the project before he started.

He was confident he could get the motor going, but the hull presented a bigger challenge, made worse by the loss of the inverter. Unable to use the 110-volt tools, he would only be able to make minor repairs. Once it was free of the sand, he intended to walk the boat around to the other side of the island. It would be easier to work on it there.

To raise the hull, he had carried over a bottle jack, several timbers, and a few sections of pipe. He went to work on the bow first as it was higher on the beach, and set a timber flat in the sand to support the jack directly below the V of the hull. This would be the hardest part of the operation as there was very little purchase for the jack against the steep angle of the hull.

With the jack set on the timber, he started pumping the steel rod, raising the head to about two inches below the point of the hull, and put a piece of wood on top of the jack to prevent the small nose from damaging the boat. Slowly he depressed the jack handle, holding the wood in place until the pressure kept it there on its own. He took a breath and jacked again, adjusting the wood slightly. This was where it would either work or not. If the wood conformed to the shape of the V hull, the jack would lift the boat enough to get a section of pipe under it.

If the wood didn't cooperate, the jack would blow out.

Again he pushed down on the jack, and the boat moved slightly. He reached over and grabbed the pipe, ready to slide it in as soon as there was enough room between the hull and the sand. One more push on the lever and the hull raised enough for him to set the pipe in place. With a wrench, he released the jack and moved it back to the flatter part of the hull he had just exposed. There he set the timber in the sand and started the procedure again. This operation would have to be repeated in two other spots on the boat, and two more pieces of pipe set, before the bottom would be free of the sand.

Once he had the pipe in place in the second spot, he replaced the plug and checked the motor tilt. The keys were still in the ignition—probably rusted there after the two years the boat had sat in one place. He turned the key, surprised at the little resistance it offered, but nothing happened - the battery was dead. The motor would have to be tilted manually. He grabbed the jack and went to the stern, where he placed it on the timber and adjusted it to a spot where the lower unit bolted to the engine, thinking this would be the fulcrum. The motor started to hinge as he jacked, and he was soon able to reach behind it and place the tilt bracket in position, securing it.

He repeated the procedure, put the third pipe in place and lifted the tools into the boat. He moved to the stern and jammed the end of a long piece of timber as far under the boat and as deep as he could into the sand and started to push, using it as a lever. At first the pipes dug in, but one at a time they started to roll, and the hull was soon floating in the clear water. Mac went around the boat, checking for damage that the sand would have concealed. There were some rough spots, but nothing appeared to be leaking. The hole in the bow was just above the water line now. The driver had grounded while on plane, when the bow was deeper in the water. But the weight of the engine with the boat at rest lowered the stern and kept the hole out of the water.

He grabbed the end of a line hooked to the bow cleat and started to pull the boat toward the other beach.

* * *

Jay leaned back in the lounge chair and sipped his drink. It was comfortable in the shade of the palapa he had built over the deck, except for the freakin' birds, which were always squawking. They were everywhere; egrets, ospreys and whatever else figured they were safe here. The constant squawking and poop were the only things that wrecked his paradise, but the wildlife sanctuary also kept boat traffic away.

The structure was nestled in the mangroves that lined the shore, giving him an element of privacy. The patio where he sat turned into a wooden dock, and was set in a small cove concealed by a series of switchbacks in the channel, making it invisible from the water.

He set the glass down on a small table next to the chair and ran his finger over the condensation. Ice was a luxury here, using a disproportionate amount of the energy that the solar system and backup generator provided. But ice made him happy, and he had forsaken air conditioning for it.

Just one more thing he'd given up for the chance to be alone and safe. His stake here was legitimate, the northwest part of the island deeded to him legally. It was reassuring, if not ironic, that the rest of the island and most of the surrounding waters were protected by the Feds. His long time affiliation with the director of the CIA had allowed him to lease this little spit of sand and brush for $99 a year, and even that was reimbursed by the CIA.

As a covert operative, he used this paradise as a base of operations for anything that could be moved by boat. That included people, guns, money, and drugs, depending on his orders. Some authorized and much not, he thought, looking over at the two boats tied to the dock. One was a twenty-two-foot single-engine center console he used to blend in with the locals, the other a forty-three-foot triple engine vessel also known as *a go fast boat*—a smuggler's dream.

He took another sip and rubbed the glass against his forehead, leaving it there for a minute to cool him as he thought about Cayenne and the casitas he'd promised to move tomorrow. Helping the girl had been a brilliant addition to his business. Lobster tails brought big money and didn't interfere with his contract work. And having her little permitted coral sanctuary—or whatever it was—so close provided the perfect cover for the casitas. The illegal traps, which could bring in one thousand tails a week at $10 per tail, added up to serious money.

For his day job, he typically ran a load or two a month, using the fast boat to take guns and cash to Cuba or Venezuela; wherever Norman Stone, director of the CIA, wanted them. The cargo brought back on the return trip was the interesting part. Pure genius on the part of Stone, who smuggled Cuban baseball players back as political refugees and took a ten percent lifetime commission on their earnings. Most of the players washed out or stayed in the minor leagues, but once in a while they hit it big.

If there was enough room in the boat, Jay filled the void with anything he could get cash for. What was the CIA going to do? He was pretty sure the work he was doing for Stone was off the books, and that gave him freedom to pursue his own agenda.

Of course, logistics were a challenge in the smuggling business. Full loads going in both directions were the way to make money, and he cursed Stone for the run he had scheduled for tomorrow. He had made a quick call to a supplier in Marathon, but they would only by able to provide a partial load of arms to deliver to his contacts there. And now Cayenne was screaming about the casitas. He picked up the phone and dialed a number from memory.

"Stone here."

"Yo, Norm, listen. We have a little schedule issue," he started.

He held the phone away from his ear as the man unleashed his usual tirade.

This wasn't the first time he'd had a scheduling conflict, and he used the fact that Stone had no choice but to deal with him to make things work to his advantage.

When the rant was over, he continued, "Got to put this off for a couple of days. Weather's bad right now, and supposed to get worse." It was the truth, but weather was usually no more than an inconvenience in his line of work. Short of a hurricane, the jobs went as scheduled. But this time he was going to make it an issue.

There was a pause, and he knew that Stone was probably at his computer, verifying what he said .

While he waited, he walked toward the dock and opened a chest freezer, removing a fish carcass and tossing it into what looked like an underwater cage with a row of barbed wire above the water. There was a large splash and the fish was gone. He smiled.

After a minute, the man's voice came back on the line. "There's no reason you can't run this cargo tomorrow."

"Norm, Norm, Norm… Listen, man. The wind stops, it takes another day for the seas to calm down. Just let them know I'll be there Thursday around dawn. I'll make the run at night."

This would give him tomorrow to pull the casitas and a few hours to play with Cayenne.

"Do I need to find someone else to run this?" the director asked.

Jay laughed. "You're going to threaten me? *Me?*" He took a

long sip of his drink, keeping the man waiting. "This is you and me, bud. I'm the only guy you have, and if you cross me I can disappear like that." He snapped his fingers. "Like vapor. You, on the other hand, will be in front of a congressional committee and above the fold of the *New York Times*."

Silence.

"So Thursday at dawn," Jay confirmed, and hung up.

He drained his drink and ambled toward the house swirling the remaining ice cubes in his mouth. At a granite topped bar he refilled the glass and went through an open living area, down a hall and to a room with three girls sprawled on a large couch under the ceiling fan. He reached for the blonde in the middle and pulled her to her feet, then led her toward his bedroom.

There were perks in running people back and forth, and this was one of them. Knowing their fates in other countries, it was hardly surprising what some of these girls would do to stay in the US. He had to keep Norm happy to keep that going.

* * *

Mel was into her second pot of coffee and deep into the charter of the non-profit when Cayenne entered the office. She glanced at the corner of the computer screen and realized it was almost 3. Cayenne nodded hello as if it was 9 in the morning and went for her office.

Most days she made a late appearance, her chest was lifted high and there was a swagger in her step. Today, her head was down. After seeing her sitting on Mac's boat yesterday, she knew why. A night in jail would do that to you. She had been furious when she had seen her and it had taken all her patience to know that a confrontation then and there would not help Mac. What she needed to do was research. Mac could scout out the area and see if he could find out anything, but if she could prove that Cayenne's non-profit was behind this it would put Mac in the clear.

Her dad had always preached to her to follow the money, and she had helped with his construction company's books through high school. Balance sheets and profit and loss statements were easy reading for her. This often gave her a distinct advantage in the legal world, where no matter how bright and witty her peers were, the ability to do simple addition was a rarity. And the numbers weren't adding up.

When she'd started having questions here, she'd done what she did best when things didn't make sense— dug into the financial statements. Numbers were more truthful than people.

The non-profit had been set up as a standard 501(c)(3). Nothing special there. An allowance for officers' salaries had been spelled out in the charter. The state of the company's books wasn't surprising in itself; non-profits often had no business plan, and were after all charities, many set up as tax shelters for their founders.

It all seemed to be above board in the beginning—several large grants and a gift from her father's foundation had financed the first two years. But the third year, things had changed. The meager coral sales in the first two years had been recorded properly, but the expenses remained high and the business was operating in the red. Then the monthly deposits in cash started flowing in, with no paperwork to back them up, along with equally large withdrawals that almost matched the deposits. It looked like money laundering on the surface, but she wanted confirmation.

The door opened and Cayenne walked out, looking defeated. "I'm going to get a drink. You want to come?"

Mel knew that there would be more than one drink, and that this might give her the opportunity she needed. "No, thanks, but go ahead."

"You shouldn't fuss about those numbers and legal stuff so much. We *are* doing good work here," Cayenne said, and walked toward her bedroom.

Mel put away the papers, not wanting to rouse suspicion, and went to the computer to check her email and wait. Before long, Cayenne emerged in a skimpy cocktail dress better suited for a twenty-year-old, the spaghetti straps barely holding her in. She said goodbye and Mel tried not to chuckle as she listened to the click clack of heels signaling her exit.

Really, heels in Key West, she thought. It was the flip-flop capital of the world.

She waited a few minutes after hearing the car start and pull out, then got up and went to Cayenne's office. The desk drawers were open and she quickly rifled through them, finding nothing interesting. Next she went to the closet and saw a small safe attached to the floor. A quick tug on the handle confirmed it was locked.

As she was about to turn away, she noticed a cardboard box marked 'taxes.' She pulled the box into the room, sat cross-legged on the floor, and started pulling out documents.

Chapter 10

The sun had just made its appearance when Jay spat in his mask and placed it over his head. A quick check of his gauges, and, with fins in hand, he stepped down the rungs of the ladder attached to the dock. His feet hit bottom and he reached over and put his fins on one at a time, then swept his arm around his right side and grabbed the regulator, stuck it in his mouth, and submerged.

Sitting below the waist-deep water was a battery-powered scooter, which he lifted out of the sand. He squeezed the trigger and the small unit pulled him through the murky water of the lagoon, around the switchbacks, and into the open water of the Gulf. This part of the trip always seemed like a Disney ride as he passed twisted mangrove roots with fish darting through them. He checked his compass and changed direction, checking his watch to estimate the distance he would travel.

He could have done this by muscle memory after so many trips, but even in the short distance to his destination, a few degrees off course and he would miss the traps. Surfacing was risky, as there were occasional boats in the area and it was unusual—but not unheard of—for the law to be prowling around out here.

When his watch hit five minutes, he started to look around. The bottom was a desert covered in turtle grass, with a few small coral heads scattered throughout. In the distance, he could just make out the line to one of the mooring balls for the coral farm. He laughed into his mouthpiece, almost choking as he took in sea water, at Cayenne's folly. But it provided the perfect cover for planting the casitas.

Once a year, some alphabet agency came down and inspected the farm, allowing plenty of notice for him to move all the structures. Otherwise, the local law enforcement generally left the area alone. He reached the first line, checked his compass again and turned ninety degrees to the north. A minute later he came to the area where the casitas should have been and looked around. In the distance he saw an irregular object standing in the sand, and used the scooter to check it out.

The trap was perpendicular to the sand, and empty. Alongside it was another, upside down on the bottom, and empty as well. He cursed into his mask knowing that someone had gotten into his traps. He had cut a deal with the desperate Cannady woman that had allowed him to place several traps in her coral farm and split the proceeds with her. They were lucrative, but he knew she was always desperate for cash. She was also the only one that knew about the traps and he suspected it was her that had cleaned them out.

He went back to the mooring line, and took another bearing. The scooter took him to the second position a minute later and he relaxed as he saw the antennas sticking out of the concrete roof. One of the things the CIA had ingrained in him was redundant systems, and he applied this to everything he did, including poaching.

He set the scooter in the sand and hovered over the bottom to approach the lightweight concrete slab elevated off the seabed with 4-inch cinder blocks. He unclipped two mesh bags and a tickle stick from his belt, and let all the air out of the BC. The negative buoyancy allowed him to hug the sand, and he got as low as he could, opened the bag, and stuck the stick into the structure.

Some lobsters retreated backwards into the deeper part of the structure, but the ones in range of the stick turned and swam tail first into the open bag. He guessed there were at least fifty in the bag, and that was only the first pass. Others scattered into the waters, beyond his reach. He let those go, knowing they would return, and moved to the next structure, where he repeated the procedure to fill the second bag.

A half hour later he grabbed the two loaded bags and clipped them to his BC. He retrieved the scooter, checked his air, and turned back toward the inlet to the cove. The original plan was to harvest what lobsters he could and then destroy the traps, but he started thinking that even if the Feds found the casitas, there was no way to tie them to *him*.

If they didn't find them, they would be full again within the week. If they did, they were in her permit area and she would be responsible. Sure, she would accuse him, but all he had to do was have Norm make a few calls and the problem would go away.

Fifteen minutes later, he reached the ladder in the lagoon, took off his fins, and hauled himself and the bags full of lobster from the water. Several thousand dollars richer. He stripped off his gear and went inside where he plucked an ice cube from the machine and put it in his mouth. While he sucked on it, he filled a glass, went to the bar and poured an amber liquid from a decanter. After he'd downed half the drink, he reached for his phone heading back outside to the deck.

A green head broke the surface of the water inside the cage as he walked towards it, but he ignored it and continued pacing the deck as the phone rang and went to voicemail.

* * *

The sun roused Mac from a sound sleep. It had taken him until sunset last night to haul the boat around the island to the small beach, where he left it tied to a pile. He had cooked the rest of the fish and, too tired for anything else, went to bed.

He swung his legs to the ground, surprised at how sore he was from pulling the boat. Then he went outside and doused himself in the rustic shower. Feeling refreshed, he headed to the beach to check on the boat. He felt an odd calm, despite his troubles. It was good to be on the island doing only what was essential to his everyday survival. *Maybe Wood had it right,* he thought as he moved aside the mangroves that disguised the trail and went towards the water. But the calm left him when he saw the boat. The island life would have to wait. Getting the engine started and repairing the hull were only the first steps to finding out what was going on at the Sawyer Keys.

It still floated, but that was about all he could say for the beaten boat. He waded out and leaned over the gunwale. Before leaving last night, he had stuffed a seat cushion in the hole, and it had held reasonably well. There was only an inch or so of water sloshing around inside the hull. He waded back toward the beach and moved the mangroves away from the skiff. It sat on a truck axle, its bow leaning forward in the sand, unbalanced since the motor was stolen. Mac took a line and tied it to the bow cleat, then started to pull, but the boat wouldn't budge. He checked the tires and found them almost flat from the couple of years since the boat had been used.

He went back to the shed and retrieved a bicycle pump and some hand tools, which he took back to the beach. It was harder than he thought to inflate the tires even to half volume, which he guessed would move them through the sand without bogging down. But soon he was able to pull the boat to the water. It floated off the axle and he tied it next to the wreck. Then he repositioned the make-shift trailer, untied the other boat, and guided it toward the waiting transport system. With the line in one hand to hold the boat in position, he went to the beach and came back with a steel cable. He attached its hook to the bow of the boat.

Now they should be ready to go.

Back on the beach, he went to the winch and started cranking. The line came taut and the boat started to move up the beach toward the clearing. He had to pause several times to catch his breath; the mechanism and axle made for a much lighter boat, but it was still a workout.

Finally, the task accomplished, he sat with his back against the wheels and rested, trying to figure out how to patch the hole. It wasn't the materials that would be the problem—he had noticed epoxy in the shed and there was plenty of wood around. But with only 12-volt power available, he wouldn't be able to use most of the tools.

He walked back to the house, pumped a jug full of water, and went to the shed. The batteries were wired in a parallel configuration, ideal for storing power at a lower voltage. By changing the connection from the current configuration of positive to positive and negative to negative, to a serial configuration of negative to positive, he thought he could gang the ten batteries together to obtain the 120 volts he needed.

The only problem would be the lack of amperage with this setup. He would have to be economical with power consumption, or the batteries would drain quickly.

One at a time, he transferred the cables, increasing the power output by 12 volts with each battery he connected. When the last battery was wired, he took the heaviest gauge extension cord he could find, cut the male end off, stripped the wires, and attached the leads to it. He eyed a drill sitting on the workbench, plugged it into the female end of the cord, and pulled the trigger.

The motor whirled to life.

Now with the power he needed, he went behind the shed and grabbed a piece of 1/4-inch plywood, hauled it to the beach, and set it by the boat. He held the board up on the outside of the hole and took a marker to outline the perimeter on the plywood. It took several trips to fit, mark, and cut, but an hour later, the piece of wood fit tightly to the hole.

The resin was a two-part mixture, which he measured into an old bucket and stirred. Unable to find any fiberglass tape for the seam, he used an old bed sheet from the house, torn into strips to bridge the connection between plywood and the hull. First he dipped the strips into the resin mixture, then applied them around the perimeter of the patch. While these dried, he applied a coat of resin with an old paint brush to the plywood to seal it.

* * *

Mel jumped and started shoving papers back in the boxes when she heard a car pull into the driveway. She kept out the two tax returns she had found and crammed the rest back in the closet. The window looked down on the driveway, and she could see a yellow mini Cooper pulling in.

She relaxed, scolding herself for both panicking and not being more attentive. Cayenne's Prius with its hybrid motor could have pulled in unnoticed, and she would have been caught in the act.

She ran from the room, grabbed her backpack, and left the house before the man could reach the front door. Signaling for him to drive, she went to the passenger seat and waited for him.

"Jeez, girlfriend. Where's my hug? What's got your panties in a wad?"

She looked over at Marvin. He would have stood out anywhere except Key West, but here he blended. His current look—unshaven, with streaks of yellow in his hair to match his car, an earring dangling from each lobe, and a nylon sweater vest over shorts—was an interesting fashion statement, but she was more interested in his brain. The reclusive accountant had retired and retreated from the city several years ago to live the Key West dream. Once a critical part of her team, his forensic accounting abilities were rivaled only by his outrageous behavior. In DC it didn't work; but here he was in heaven.

"Love you, too." She punched him on the arm. "How's tricks?"

"Funny you should ask. But that little bit of gossip can wait for a cocktail."

"Let's get out of here. You help me with this and I'll be your wingman later."

He put the car in reverse and backed out of the driveway. "Where to?"

She thought for a moment about where they would be safe. "How about the library?"

"Woohoo - Sounds like a hot date!" He made several turns, ending up on White Street, and then turned left on Flemming. They parked and walked into the air-conditioned lobby.

"Let's go find a quiet spot," Mel said as they entered.

She steered clear of the rows of homeless-looking people pecking away at ancient computers by the door and led him to an empty table.

"OK, sweet cheeks, tell old Marvin all your troubles."

Mel started with a brief history of Coral Gardens.

"Cayenne Cannady … you mean Big Boobs Cannady?"

"Yeah, that's her." She waited for him to elaborate.

"Sweetie, that girl has issues, and if tell you someone has issues …" He put his hands out.

Mel wasn't sure she wanted to hear about Cayenne's seedier side, at least not until they'd had a few drinks. Knowing your enemy was one of the crucial tenants of her success and she didn't fail to notice that this was the first time she had referred to her that way.

Trying to get the conversation out of the gutter, she took the papers from her backpack and laid them on the table for him. As soon as the IRS letterhead on the tax forms caught his eye, his interest perked. For several minutes he shuffled papers, going back and forth in the stack after sorting them into their appropriate years.

Finally he looked up. "Seems our girl runs her business about the same as her sex life—sloppy, sweetheart, sloppy, sloppy, sloppy."

Mel was getting impatient. Marvin must have sensed it, because he continued in a serious tone. "The books are cooked to about a medium-well, but that's not really the issue." He tapped the pile of financials. "These are unaudited statements and pretty much worthless in a court of law. The tax returns, on the other hand—" He tapped a tax form. "This is Form 990, filed by non-profits." He turned the page to section A and put his index finger on line 5. "Here's the deal. This line is for what the IRS calls significant diversions. Non-profits are typically money sieves. All full of good intentions, but nobody's counting the pennies, or even watching the dollars. Fraud and theft are common, but the IRS chooses not to ask questions. Line 5 here is where they ask if anything has been stolen … for any reason."

He pulled out the previous year and put the returns side by side. "Two years in a row, the number here matches the cash withdrawals. As long as you fill in the paperwork correctly no one cares, so I'm guessing no one checked up on this."

"You mean she's admitting to taking money?" Mel asked.

"No. Her accountant is talking to the IRS through this line, saying that something has disappeared, but he's not sure what it is. Just enter the figure there and every one walks away, no questions asked."

Mel stared at the papers and the sizable figure entered. It's money laundering. Taking the cash for the lobsters and putting it into the account, then withdrawing it. "What about all the cash deposits with no paperwork?"

"Nothing there—it's a dead end. As long as they are under ten grand." He scanned the journal. "And they are. So the IRS could care less about reporting income. If they were more than ten thousand, the banks would report the transaction and it might raise a red flag. But not here."

She had a lot to digest, and clearly owed him an hour or so as his wingman. Fortunately, from experience, she knew it wouldn't take much more than that to get him hooked up. Her phone showed 5 o'clock. If she got rid of him in an hour, she would have plenty of time to rent a stand-up paddleboard and if the wind held, get some downwind time. A good paddle would clear her head and put things in perspective. The pieces were there, she just had to put them together.

"Well, girlfriend. I guess it's party time."

Chapter 11

Trufante hadn't moved from the barstool for several hours, and his brain—as well as his credit—were both close to maxed out. He put the stub of his missing finger against the cold bottle to cool it down. Whenever he got stressed out, this was the first place he felt it, and right now it was burning. Of all the things he could have gotten sucked into, this was about the worst case scenario. He was used to living life in DEFCON 2.5 but this was looking like an Armageddon fuck-up.

But losing Mac's boat because of a woman, with a handful of greed tossed in, was about the worst thing he had ever done. Besides breaching his friend's trust and lying about taking the boat, he'd managed to get his vessel impounded, and in an island community, boats were more important than cars. Especially when both of their incomes relied on it.

The next thing they would do, if they hadn't gotten there already, was pull Mac's commercial license. Then they would be two broke homeboys.

He shook his head and finished the beer, wondering if the woman behind the bar would extend his credit for one more. Before he could ask, someone smacked him on the shoulder. His reaction was slowed from the night in jail and the beer, and when he turned he saw a gold smile staring at him.

"Trufante."

"Commando. Son of a bitch." He fist bumped the man, who moved to the empty barstool.

Commando pulled up his low riding shorts and pushed his wide-brimmed cap back on his head. "Yo, Tru. How 'bout we get you a beer?"

Trufante smiled at his luck. Commando had a small fleet of boats that went out in the mornings for bait. It wasn't the highest-paying work around, and nothing like the generous split that Mac gave him, but any kind of work right now was good. "That'd be good, man."

They sat and waited for the beers to arrive. When she set them down, he held up a finger for her to wait.

"You want a shot too?" Commando didn't wait for an answer. "Two tequilas."

After the barmaid poured the shots, they toasted and downed them before each took a sip of beer. Commando broke the silence. "So, word on the street is that you and the man got in a little bit of trouble."

Trufante looked at him and shook his head. "Damn shit, if you ask me. Feds took his boat for some stupid thing he wasn't even there for."

"That doesn't put either of you in a very good position, does it?" His gold teeth showed as he smiled.

Trufante looked at him, trying to decide where this was going. Mac didn't like the man. He always said that the second- and third-generation Cubans who wore their pants low and inked up there bodies had no respect; that they were punks. Trufante knew there was some history with Commando and the law, but he was standing here and buying beers. The least he could do was hear him out, and maybe get another beer out of him.

"You got something on your mind?" He drained the beer.

Commando signaled down the bar for a replacement. "*Mi amigo*. Maybe I can help you both out, here. You know, I hear things. Heard you scored big the other day."

Trufante waited for the beer. "Come on, man, spit it out. You know Mac don't care for you."

"That's a nice way to put it, but I can help both of you. They're probably going to pull his license any minute now, and without the license and boat ..." He paused. "It's lobster season, and if his traps are bringing in numbers like I heard you scored yesterday, I'd be willing to cut him in for his numbers and equipment."

Trufante looked at him, waiting for the rest.

"And there'd be a pretty large finder's fee in it for you. Work too, if you want."

Trufante soaked up the offer with another sip of beer. It wasn't a bad deal really, and probably the only one Mac would get. He didn't guess there was any point in telling him about the casitas, though—that would just devalue the offer. Let him keep thinking that everything came from their traps.

"Well?" Commando motioned for two more beers.

"Tried calling his cell before, but it went right to voicemail. Texted him too, but it didn't go through. Bet he's out at old Wood's place. Phone's probably gone dead."

Commando raised his glass to toast. "So do we have a deal, then?"

Trufante reluctantly tapped bottles. "It ain't my deal to make, but I'll take a ride out there with you and see what he says."

* * *

It was late in the afternoon by the time Mac got the second coat of resin sanded. He eyed the patch; not his best work, but it looked like it would hold water. The rest of the hull had been inspected, and although it was dinged up pretty badly, he didn't see any obvious leaks or weak spots.

While the resin had dried, he'd started work on the engine. The prop still turned, reassuring him that it wasn't frozen, which would make the engine unrepairable. One piece at a time, he took the lower unit apart, spreading the parts on a tarp he brought from the shed. Once separated, he cleaned and lubricated each one before reassembling the unit.

Now he moved on to the motor, first draining the oil and checking the flywheel. There was no new oil in the shed so he went to Wood's jug of old oil and used that. The old man had been religious about oil changes, and his used oil looked much better than what had come out of the engine after sitting for two years.

Just as he was about to check the battery and fuel, he heard the rumble of a boat in the distance. He reached down for his jug of water and scanned the horizon. As he drank, he watched a small dot turn into the outline of a boat, and then become a cigarette boat.

It was coming right at the beach, and he wondered if he shouldn't go grab Wood's shotgun from the house. Then the boat veered around a sandbar known only to a few locals. He looked again, shading his eyes against the sun, and saw the unmistakeable grin on the man sitting in the passenger seat. Besides his six-foot-plus height and long blonde hair, Trufante had a smile that closely resembled the grill of a Cadillac. Mac recognized it immediately.

The boat came closer and slowed as they reached the lone pile. When it stopped, Trufante slid over the side with a rope in hand and tied it off. Mac was looking at the boat and its driver when he noticed several crates piled against the transom. Trufante distracted him when he vaulted the gunwale and landed in the water.

"Yo, Mac. What's shakin'?" Trufante asked as he waded toward the beach where Mac stood staring at the boat.

"You're the last person I want to see and whatcha bring him out for?" Mac asked, his voice low so as not to be heard by the man waiting in the boat.

"Shoot. Ain't no way to say hey." Trufante patted his back.

"'Shoot' is what I ought to do to you. Don't you realize this is all your fault?" Mac was close to losing his temper at the mild-mannered Cajun.

"Ok. I got that. But hear the dude out. He's got an offer that could help us both."

Mac squinted into the sun at the man on the boat. "Nothing he has to say is going to help me." He turned to his work and started fiddling with the engine. Commando was trouble. Came from a family of trouble that had somehow run every bait fisherman out of town. He was so angry that Trufante had brought him here, and was concentrating so hard on the engine, that tunnel vision took over, preventing him from hearing the man approach.

Mac jumped back, startled.

"No worries, man. I just want to talk," Commando said.

"Did anyone give you permission to set foot on this beach? It might be the middle of nowhere, but it's still private property."

He backed into the water. "Mean high tide is public. Mind if I stand here?"

"Guess not." He shrugged in resignation. The only way the man was leaving was at gunpoint, or if Mac heard him out. Feeling cornered, he said, "You can state your business from there."

Commando stood in the knee-deep water. "Do I need to restate your situation? It's only a matter of time until Fish and Game suspends your license on top of all the other shit you stepped in."

Mac looked down at the engine in pieces on the tarp, thinking it resembled his life right now.

Commando picked up on his body language. "I guess you didn't think all this through." His gold tooth glinted in the sun.

Mac looked at him warily. "Go on. What do you have to say?"

"I can help you out here. Just give me your permission and the GPS numbers for your strings and I'll take them over. Give you ten percent off the top. This is going to take you months to clear up, and they're gonna be watching you even if your ass doesn't end up in jail. You leave those traps untended all winter and they'll be trashed by March when the season closes."

Mac knew the man was probably right, but there was no way he was giving in this easily. "I'll take my chances."

"Whatever. Got an errand to run I'm leaving dufus with you." He started wading towards the boat and turned back, "Change your mind, and I guess you will, the deal stands."

Mac could only guess what kind of an errand he would have to run out here and looked back at the crates on the boat. Smuggling. If it would get Commando off his beach he would deal with Trufante. "Well, come on. You got me in this mess. The least you can do is help get this thing started." He walked back to the boat. A minute later the engines started and he heard the boat pull away.

Trufante walked over to the hull. "That's the boat that boy wrecked out here and almost killed Wood with,"

Mac ignored him, reached over the side, and tried the key. Silence prevailed, and he smacked the steering wheel. "Yeah, it is. Go back to the shack and get a battery off the solar system. I'll deal with the fuel."

Trufante disappeared down the path and Mac went to the motor-less skiff. He looked into the cockpit, but the gas can was gone as well. Must have been stolen with the motor, he thought as he went to the bushes and pulled a red can from the clutches of the mangroves. Back at the boat, he cut a beer can that he had found on the boat in half and poured gas from the red can into it.

From the color, he was sure that there was oil in the gas—ready for use in the two-cycle engine. He waited a few minutes to see if a layer of water would show as the mixture settled. It looked good, and he was about to pour it back in the can when he heard a loud boom.

He ran toward the house and saw a smoke cloud coming out of the shed. It cleared as he got closer, and he watched Trufante stumble out of the building with a battery held between his hands.

"Shit. Didn't tell me you had the sucker wired for 110."

Mac just shook his head. The shock he had probably taken was only a fraction of what he deserved. "Give me that." He took the heavy marine battery from the Cajun. "I got it, go get yourself cleaned up."

Trufante headed for the hose behind the building while Mac took the battery down the path to the beach. His arms burning from its weight, he put it into the cockpit of the boat and sat on one of the wheels to catch his breath.

A few minutes later, he climbed over the side and hooked up the battery that he hoped had a full charge from the solar system. Next he hooked up the gas tank, opened the vent, and primed the bulb. The only thing that might stop the boat from starting was a gummed-up carburetor, but with the motor sitting at the angle it had been, he expected the gas had drained out of the bowl before it could evaporate, leaving the solids that caused engine trouble.

Trufante reappeared, shirtless, just as he was about to try and start the engine. Mac turned the key and the starter engaged, but the engine refused to start. He pushed the key in to open the choke and tried again.

This time it coughed.

The lower unit would need water to cool the engine, but he could get a sense of the condition of the engine with a dry start. One more time, and the motor sounded like it might start. But he'd have to get the lower unit into the water before he would know for sure.

Chapter 12

Mel had to admit she was having a good time, despite her regret over not paddling tonight. She sat next to Marvin at the open air bar, soaking in the atmosphere and the rum drinks in front of them. Though not much of a drinker, she had to admit the day's special was really good. The mixture of cucumber, lime juice, rum, and ginger beer was going down fast; she was almost through her first and Marvin was cruising through his third when she looked at the mirror behind the bar and saw a flash of red hair walk through the door.

"Shit. That's her," she said as low as she could, over the music.

He peered around her toward the door. "Yes it is, and her boobies are leading the way." He giggled and sucked more of the concoction through the straw. "Chin up, sweetie. Here she comes."

"Why Mel, look at you," Cayenne said as she slid aside the empty stool and stood next to Marvin. She pecked his cheek and looked toward the bartender.

"Cayenne Cannady. Don't you look delicious," Marvin said as he finished the drink and set the empty glass on the bar top. "Sweetie, you've got to try one of these."

"Didn't think I'd see you in a place like this," Cayenne said to Mel after she ordered a round.

Mel ignored the barb. "Marvin here is an old friend from

DC. I promised to be his wing man for a while," she said, nursing the rest of her drink. "Oh we can get our boy here hooked up. What fun!" Cayenne said as she drained her glass and looked at Mel. "Going to drink that?"

Mel nodded no and Cayenne reached for the glass. She was getting uncomfortable; not because of the surroundings, but because of the company, which had her on edge. Given an hour and a crowded bar, she could easily have fulfilled her obligation and had Marvin dancing with the boy toy of his choice, but looking over at the grotesque figure of Cayenne, she knew the task would not be so easy now. Even the pot-bellied, middle-aged tourists ignored her.

She looked toward the street, trying to estimate how much daylight was left, and whether she had enough time to ditch the pair and get her paddle in. But the sun was already blocked by the building across the street. Resigned to her fate, she raised her hand to attract the bartender and ordered another round. There was always the chance that she could get her companions drunk enough they wouldn't notice her exit.

* * *

The tires crunched in the sand as the boat slid backwards into the water. As soon as the bow splashed the axle came free and Mac had Trufante hold it in place while he slid the boat off. He stood in the water as Trufante hooked the old axle to the winch cable and cranked it back onto the beach.

"Here." He tossed him the line. "Hold onto her. I'll get in and see if she runs." He jumped onto the gunwale and pulled himself into the boat. At the helm, he closed his eyes, willing his energy into the wiring, depressed the ignition, and turned the key.

The motor coughed and died.

He tried again, this time without pressing the key in to open the choke. The motor spun, and just as he was about to turn the key off, kicked to life. A large black cloud floated behind the boat as he pressed the throttle and gave it gas. He backed off and let the engine idle. It was a little rough, and he would probably have to clean the plugs, but it was serviceable.

"Come on," he yelled to Trufante, and waited while he tossed the line in the bow and hopped in. Gently he pulled back on the throttle, cringing as the gears ground against each other as they tried to shift the transmission into reverse. He gave a little gas, but the boat hesitated, as if it had forgotten what to do. Finally it started to move backwards through the water.

"I'm gonna run it for a bit. Can you watch the patch in the bow and check the bilge for water?"

He didn't wait for an answer and pushed the throttle forward. But the boat jumped and died.

"Shit," he mumbled as he pulled back on the throttle and set the boat in neutral. It restarted easily, and this time when he punched the throttle down it reacted and pushed through the water. He looked at Trufante for confirmation that all was good, and got the boat on plane.

Cruising at about 25 knots, he started to test the steering, turning the boat in quick right and left turns. It was a little sticky at first, but soon the self-lubricating cable connecting the helm to the engine did its job and the boat turned easily. Next he started to circle, submerging the patch into the sea. This would be a true test, to see if it was water tight with the added pressure of the water from the boat's forward momentum. Satisfied, he pulled back on the throttle and the boat coasted to a stop, bobbing as the wake passed by it.

"Looks good," Trufante said.

"For now. Still going to have to pull the plugs and clean her up," Mac said. He was exhilarated from the ride; the feeling of taking a wrecked boat and fixing it had temporarily put his problems from his mind.

Now he looked at Trufante, and they came flooding back.

"That place where you pulled those tails. It's not far, is it?"

"Nope." Trufante smiled.

* * *

Norm Stone looked around the well-appointed office, wishing he wasn't there. Every day he spent in the confines of the Langley, Virginia headquarters of the CIA killed him a little at a time. Walking past the statue of Wild Bill Donovan dressed in his fatigues made him yearn to get back in the field. An administrator he was not, and had been surprised when the president asked him to take the position several months ago, and even *more* surprised when Congress had given him a pass and confirmed his nomination.

Maybe they were scared of blowback by rejecting the first Cuban-American nominee for a major office. Whatever the reason, which he suspected to be tied to the president's agenda for Cuba, he was miserable.

He stood and looked at the pictures on his wall. A few were of family, but many were baseball players. One of the only perks about being stuck in the office was finally having a permanent residency and season tickets to the Washington Nationals. The team was in the hunt this year, and desperately needed a late inning relief pitcher. The Nationals had only made the playoffs twice since 1969, but this year looked promising ... if they could only straighten out their bullpen, they could make a playoff run. With salary cap woes on the mound, the team was stuck, but Norm had a solution. In the past he had been a little more speculative on the players he smuggled out of Cuba. He knew if he went after the big names that Castro's watchdogs would notice. But by taking lesser-known players with promise, he had stayed under the radar.

The problem was that evaluating talent in Cuba was hard. They didn't have the competition that even the single-A ball leagues had here. You never knew if they would make it or not.

Pitchers were even more of a gamble, as they typically got less rest and, as a result, barely broke the coveted 90-mph mark for their fastballs.

But all said, skimming ten percent off their salaries was making him money. And the information he had on his desk—for a new player—was higher profile than most of the players he dealt with. Which meant it would surely be noticed when he went missing.

But the reward was worth the risk—especially if he could save the Nationals' season.

He got up and paced the room, ignoring the view. Then picked up his cell phone, hit the icon for Snapchat, and typed in the message to Jay. Upon delivery, the message would be scrubbed from both his phone and the server. The irony made him smile, how an app developed for teenagers had revolutionized the espionage business.

A minute later, the phone chirped and he looked at the reply: *Tonight—loading now.* The junior man had worked for him for years, and was a good operative, although he had tendencies to go off the rails occasionally - especially when women were involved. But he was the only one Stone trusted to run the off-the-books operation in Cuba, running guns and money to the island state and bringing back political refugees and players.

Norm didn't understand a large part of the world—something else that troubled him about his appointment—but two things he did understand were Cuba and baseball. A second generation American, his parents had left Cuba in the late 50s, right before Castro took over, and had instilled in him a love for the country and an equal love for the sport. Why not hurt the regime at the same time as putting some money in his pocket and helping his team?

He wished he was back in the field and could control the operation himself. Both Jay and the man he used to extricate the players, were becoming increasingly difficult to control from behind his desk. The man named Alvarez, had grown up on the island, and emigrated in the Mariel boat lift of the early 1980s. Over the years he had performed well, but had grown accustomed to the vices of a capitalist society and Norm was hesitant to send him back. Alvarez was becoming unpredictable, but he had the connections and local knowledge to sneak into the country and bring the players out. And Jay was Jay - he needed to be watched.

He thought for a second about how he would justify the expense. As head of the CIA, there was no way he could drop off the grid - at least as himself. He lifted the phone to ask his secretary to call for his plane to be ready and file a flight plan to the Marathon airport, but hung up before she answered. After unlocking the bottom drawer of his desk, he pulled out a passport and ID in another name and placed them in his pocket. Better to go off the grid for this trip.

Relieved that he had decided to take action, he left the office and headed out of the building, once again passing the statue of Wild Bill and wondering why this couldn't be more like the old days before congressional hearings and bullshit inquisitions. He often felt powerless to make any kind of change in the world, but with the Nationals there just might be a chance.

* * *

Mel was getting more uncomfortable as the bar filled. Cayenne and Marvin were engrossed in a conversation, neck and neck, sucking down rum drinks, and she was left to the side, watching the crowd. They were getting louder and more animated as they drank and she was starting to get a headache. She had tried to leave several times, but Marvin had ordered another drink and reminded her of her promise to hook him up.

She tapped him on the shoulder. "Hey. I can't be your wingman if you're going to sit there and talk to her all night. I'm getting a headache."

"Oh, sweetie. Don't get bitchy. Maybe we could get a bite to eat and that would make you feel better. Then we can cruise for some boys."

"Deal. At least the first part." She got up from the stool and went for the door. When she reached the entrance, she turned and saw that Cayenne was following like a little puppy.

Why me? she thought as the trio decided on the Half-Shell Oyster Bar. They walked along Duval Street and turned onto Caroline, where they marched the four blocks in the early evening heat to the restaurant. The air conditioning was almost non-existent as they entered and walked past the bar, crowded with charter captains whose boats were moored behind the restaurant at the Key West Bight Marina. The rustic bar, with its happy hour specials on both drinks and seafood, was a popular after-charter watering hole.

A man nodded at her as she passed. She thought he looked familiar, but couldn't place him, so she looked away and followed the hostess to their table by the open windows. A few minutes later she sat with a glass of ice water, peeling shrimp and watching the animated conversation going on between Marvin and Cayenne. They were gulping beer and slurping oysters, a large part of the juice falling into Cayenne's overgrown cleavage.

When Marvin went to lick it off Mel got up and excused herself.

After a quick trip to the ladies' room, which she had only used as an excuse to get away, she stopped at the bar to check her phone. Mac still hadn't called or texted and she was starting to get worried. It wasn't unusual for him to disappear, and he was not one to just say *hi*, but it had been almost forty-eight hours since they'd parted. She should have gotten some kind of message.

The man at the bar was still there and she covertly studied his face, trying to remember where she knew him from.

It finally came to her as she started to walk away that he was the captain of the boat that had taken them to the coral farm.

Chapter 13

The light was fading fast and Mac flipped the toggle switch for the running lights on the off chance they would still work. Surprisingly, they did. It was a bit of good news, as a vessel without lights was both dangerous and suspicious. The boat had run well so far, and they had gone by a couple of his traps to pick up some lobsters. He still had his license, and before he was forced to abandon his gear, or worse, make a deal with Commando, he might as well fill up the freezer.

He looked down at his blistered hands. They had pulled about twenty lobster from a half dozen of his traps without the aid of a winch, and having to handle the lines—encrusted with crustaceans—without gloves had torn their hands apart.

"How far to that spot?" he asked as half the sun dipped below the horizon, the other half following swiftly behind it.

Trufante pointed to a small island in the distance. "Over there."

The Sawyer Keys were only a mile away, close enough to make before they lost daylight. Mac put the boat in gear and was quickly on plane, following Trufante's signals and trusting the Cajun wouldn't run them aground. The man had a way of getting in trouble, but he was good on the water. Minutes later, they arrived by one of the buoys. He had grilled the Cajun about his day with the red-headed woman and hoped if he saw the operation for himself he could figure out a way out of his mess. "So this girl is growing coral here?" he asked.

"Yup, ain't seen that part of the operation, but them casitas were over there." Trufante pointed toward a spot in between two other buoys.

"Wish I had some dive gear. I'd like to take a look and see what's got me in so much trouble," Mac said as he started searching the boat, looking for a mask and fins. Finding nothing except some empty beer cans, he closed the hatches and went back to the wheel. Just as he was about to start the motor, though, he stopped.

"What?" Trufante asked.

Mac put a finger to his lips. Trufante started to ask again when the sound of an engine stopped him. They both scanned the horizon, looking for the source, and finding nothing. Suddenly a cigarette boat appeared from a clump of mangroves less than a hundred yards from them.

"Down." Mac pulled Trufante to the deck with him.

"What?"

"It's Commando. Hard to believe it's a coincidence that he's right here, but I don't want him to see us." Mac raised his head and peered over the transom. "Looks like he's gone." He rose and looked at the boat speeding toward Big Pine Key. "Pretty dark and it's not my boat. I don't think he saw us. Or if he did, he didn't recognize us."

"Probably going back to pick me up," Trufante said.

"Wrong way, buddy. Looks like he ditched you. I think you're stuck with me 'till morning. If he even comes back. Running that boat of his at night is a bullseye for the law to come after him."

"Well, what now?"

Mac looked at the clump of mangroves where Commando's boat had emerged. He was curious; from this vantage point there was no place for a boat to exit. "Let's go have a look at where he came from. This is all too much of a coincidence for my liking. First the casitas, and now Commando."

He went to the wheel and pushed the throttle forward. At idle speed, he moved closer to the mangroves, one eye on the depth finder, the other on the shore. They reached the spot he was sure the cigarette boat had emerged from, but all he could see was mangroves.

As they got closer, a small light became visible through the branches, and then a small inlet suddenly appeared. It was barely wide enough for a single boat and looked deep, like it had been dredged. He passed the inlet to look from the other side, and it vanished. The light was low now, but he could see in his mind the artfully crafted entrance. Cut parallel to the shore line and deep enough for a single boat to enter and turn, it would look like a small cove from one angle, and be virtually invisible from any other. Perfectly hidden.

Mac swung the boat around and headed toward the entrance.

"What are you doin'?" Trufante asked.

"I'm going to see what's in there. This is professionally done, especially for a Key's camouflage job." The backwaters of the Keys were legendary for smuggling whatever the current rage was: liquor from Cuba during prohibition, drugs for the last fifty years, and whatever else was in vogue and illegal in between. Smugglers and pirates had holed up in these mangrove-covered, mosquito-infested islands and unmarked flats for centuries.

"It's got to have something to do with the casitas," he told Trufante. "And the only way I'm gong to clear my name and get my boat back is to figure this out myself."

"I'm just sayin', this was the bayou, you don't go unannounced, or unarmed into a spot like this."

"This is the perfect cover. Two tourists lost in a rental boat." Mac followed the small inlet and turned right at the blind turn, which switchbacked onto another narrow pass. "Someone spent some money doing this."

"Well if they spent money building it, don't you think they'd spend money guarding it?" Trufante whined.

Mac steered through the second turn and found himself in a small lagoon. A dock jutted out into the water, where another cigarette boat and a smaller center console were tied up. In the background he could make out a dimly lit house.

Satisfied for now, he started to turn away. But suddenly a gun fired, and he felt the whistle of a bullet flying by his head. Trufante was already on the deck when he pushed back on the throttle, reversed and spun the boat. He slammed the throttle forward hoping the engine could take the sudden shock and sped through the tight turns. Several shots followed, but they were increasingly off target and he relaxed as they hit open water. He turned the running lights off and headed toward deeper water, wanting to put as much distance between them and the gunman as quickly as possible.

They reached the channel leading to Wood's place fifteen minutes later, and he had Trufante tie off the boat to the piling. It was starting to look crowded here with both boats and he worried it might attract attention. The motor-less skiff was tied to the pile as well and he thought about putting it up on the trailer to hide it but decided it wasn't worth the effort. If someone had followed them he would have to hide both boats, but he had seen no pursuit. Tired and hungry now, he looked at the buckets on the deck.

"Let's go cook some of these up. Be nice to have a cold beer, too." He hopped over the gunwale and dropped into the water, his cut hands stinging when he grabbed the buckets of lobster from Trufante.

"Maybe this'll work," Trufante said as he slid into the water holding a half-full bottle of rum above his head. "You only found the empties. Me, I can sniff this out from a mile away."

* * *

Mel looked around the bar and was about to turn and talk to the captain about running her out to Mac's. The hours were ticking by and still no call or message from him. Just as she was about to catch his eye, Marvin grabbed her arm and pulled her away.

"Sweetie, let's go get some guys," he said, jerking her away from the bar.

She looked over at the man, but he had turned the other way. "I'll give you an hour." She went to the door, ready to pay off her obligation when Cayenne came running through the bar, boobs bouncing and tripping on her heels. "Do I really need to deal with her?"

"You were the one looking for information. Ply her with alcohol and I'll bet you'll learn something. If not, just throw her in front of the first tourist with a Rolex that comes along and she'll be gone," Marvin said as he held the door open for the women.

Mel was glad to be out of the bar. "Where to, then? Clock's ticking."

He gave her a look like she was clueless. "Aqua on Duval," he said, and started toward Duval Street.

"That place is so cool," Cayenne said as she chased after them. She held up a hand and flagged a cab. The pink car pulled to the curb and they got into the air-conditioned interior. "Time's a wasting, and I can't walk in these things."

Mel sat back and watched the scenery as the old Victorian homes turned into T-shirt shops and restaurants. *There must be a cruise ship in port*, she thought as she watched the masses of people wandering the sidewalk. Several blocks later, they pulled up to a turquoise art deco building illuminated with neon in the fading twilight. Cayenne paid the driver, and they exited the cab and headed toward the open doors.

Both bars adjacent to the doors were full, and she waited as Marvin scanned the crowd. She looked at the handful of bodies on the dance floor and wondered if she could really get him hooked up and out of here in the hour she had threatened. Her head started to throb again from the rum drinks, made worse by the pulsing music coming from the back of the club. Marvin was looking back and forth like a kid scanning a candy display until finally he chose and headed toward the larger bar on the right, where he took an empty stool and sat.

"What's with you?" she yelled in his ear. "You can't just sit here and make me do all the work." Mel looked at him and noticed his body language had changed. Gone was the cocky guy she had watched earlier. In his place was a nervous boy.

"I get a little nervous lately, doing this kind of thing."

"I can see that. OK. I promised. You order a drink and let me see what I can do." She walked down the bar, trying not to look intimidating. Some women caught her eye in an attempt to communicate, but the men ignored her. At the end of the bar, she spotted Cayenne leaning into a man sitting by himself and moved toward them. The man was obviously a tourist, and here alone. *Perfect,* she thought. Now all she had to do was to pry Cayenne's boobs off his chest.

"Aren't you James?" she asked the man as she approached and winked.

"Who me?" he answered, trying to extricate himself from Cayenne.

Mel was about to give up the ploy when he must have figured out that she was here to help.

"I know you. From that conference last fall," he said, appearing to catch on. He pushed Cayenne to the side and went to Mel.

They exchanged air kisses and she leaned over and whispered in his ear, "Name's Mel. I'll help you out here if you let me introduce you to my friend down there." She pointed at Marvin, then turned and faced Cayenne. "You know the guys in here don't want to play with you, right?"

Cayenne pushed past her and stormed out of the bar. Mel walked the man toward Marvin, who looked awfully nervous sitting by himself sipping a drink.

"Hey Marvin," she said.

He looked up and smiled. "Sweetie. What have you brought your friend?"

"You two have a little chat, OK? I'm going to see what Cayenne is up to."

* * *

The boat was packed and the load covered, ready to leave, when Jay saw the boat enter the cove. It wasn't the first time tourists had wandered in here, but a few shots wouldn't hurt to keep them from getting too curious. He ran to the house and retrieved his rifle from the safe in his office, ran back out, and let loose on the boat, purposefully aiming high. Maybe he'd get one of those annoying birds, and he didn't want any dead bodies floating around before he had to take off. The boat picked up speed and disappeared.

He had one last thing to handle and he would be out of here. The palm trees rustled overhead and he looked up at a large cumulous cloud illuminated in the moonlight. With a new urgency, he walked into the house and went toward the bedroom. The last thing he wanted was to start the trip in a storm. From the look of the cloud and the direction of the breeze, he had a good thirty minutes before it got here. Once he was underway he could easily outrun it.

He set his hand on the doorknob and took a deep breath before he turned it and entered the room. This was going to be a fight, and he had no time for it with weather approaching. Of all the cargo he had hauled over all the years, the human variety was always the most dangerous and unpredictable.

Soft light lit the room and three girls were strewn over

cushions on the floor, in various stages of undress. A man rolled from in between two of them when the door slammed.

"What the fuck?" the naked man exclaimed.

"What the fuck is this? Put your clothes on and say goodbye. Time to go," Jay said as he reached behind his back and pulled a gun from the waistband of his shorts. The man had been here less than a day and already he was trouble.

"Easy now, Jefe," the man said with a Spanish accent. "I was only having a little fun."

Jay kept the gun pointed at the naked man. Although he was not a threat, the gun moved things along nicely. Without it, they would be here bickering for another five minutes. "There's a storm coming. Unless you want to spend ninety miles puking over the side, I suggest that we get on with it. Now put on your pants and say goodbye." He waved the gun for emphasis.

The man got the message and reluctantly got up and reached for his pants.

"Not those. You need to go native. No American anything. It all stays here."

"Shit," the man said as he covered himself with the pants and left the room.

Jay nodded to the girls, who smiled back, probably thankful he wasn't taking them. They knew that as bad as their incarceration here, it could be a lot worse. He followed the man into the bedroom down the hall and waited at the door as he dug through a box of clothes on the closet floor before extracting several old and worn garments from the pile. With the gun still pointed at him, he dressed.

The men left the house and walked down the dock toward the boat. Jay waited while he boarded, then climbed in himself, gun still in hand. He went to the wheel and started the engines. The three 275-hp Yamaha four strokes started immediately. Jay motioned for the man to untie the dock lines and waited, checking the water outlet on the engines to make sure they were cooling properly. The man returned to the leaning post by the wheel and braced himself. Jay took another look at the cloud, now much closer than before, the wind fresher, and pushed the three throttles forward.

He kept the boat at an idle until he cleared the last switchback, then accelerated into the night. Within seconds the boat was on plane, and he checked the tachometers. Slight adjustments were made to each throttle until each engine was running at 4400 rpms. Then he checked the GPS screen for direction and speed.

Although he knew the route by heart, running at 45 mph through the back country at night was not an easy task. There were several small islands and shoals he would have to avoid before he reached water deep enough to relax.

Chapter 14

Mel ran out of the club and looked both ways, searching the crowd for Cayenne. Duval Street was loud and crowded with both locals and tourists prowling the bars for action. Street vendors peddled their wares, forcing some of the partiers onto the street, where bicycles, scooters, and cars swerved to avoid them. She was tall enough to see over the throng, and scanned the crowds again. Anywhere else but Key West and Cayenne's distinctive hair and features would have stood out, but in the heart of Duval, they blended in perfectly.

She turned in the direction of Mallory Square and the cruise ship pier, taking a chance that Cayenne had gone toward the busier end of the street. After walking a few blocks and with no idea where the woman went, or even why she was following, she gave up and turned around. She didn't particularly want to go back to the bar, but she owed Marvin a goodbye, and had to admit she was curious to see how her matchmaking skills had turned out.

Before she went in, she checked her phone, hoping to see a message from Mac. But the screen was empty and she wondered again if he was all right. A tear formed in her eye, which she wiped away. Just as she braced herself to walk back into the bar, Marvin ran out, almost knocking her to the ground.

She regained her balance and looked at his tear-streaked face.

"What's up? I've never seen you behave like that. You're usually the life of the party." She waited patiently while he breathed and tried to control his emotions.

"It's a long story. But sweetie, why are you crying?"

"It's nothing. Just missing Mac," she replied. "I'm starting to think something might have happened to him."

"Well maybe we can help each other. I can use some fresh air. How about we get out of here and take a ride to see your boyfriend."

"That's really sweet, but he's on an island out in the backcountry—my dad's old place."

He smiled. "All the better. I have a boat. If you can get us there, I'd be happy to go. My skin is crawling."

She gave him a questioning look, "What's going on with you?"

"I'll tell you on the way," he said and started walking.

She followed him as he turned down a side street and walked several blocks. There he reached into his pocket for the car keys and hit the unlock button on the fob.

Mel was not about to question him. If she had a ride out to the island, she was going to take it. She knew the waters well enough to get there in the dark.

* * *

"What's got into you? Ain't no gator gonna bite your ass the way you're movin' around." Trufante held the bottle of rum in one hand and a lobster tail in the other.

Mac paced the clearing, getting more agitated by the moment. "Get up. We're going back there."

"Back where?" Trufante slurred, glancing at the inch of liquor remaining in the bottle.

"To the island. We're going in the back way. Whoever that is, or whatever is going on there, has something to do with this mess you've got me in."

"Now?" Tru took a sip from the bottle and chewed the last bite of meat.

"Night is best, especially after getting shot at today. There's a small beach on the other side of the island that we can land on at low tide." Mac looked at the sky, the full moon hanging low on the horizon. "Ought to give us enough light to see, and the tide will be down, too."

"Shit." Trufante swatted a mosquito and finished the bottle. "Think these bad boys are bad here. Wait 'till we get in the mangroves over there."

"I got a cure for that. Now get moving." Mac didn't wait for an answer. He walked toward the shed and came out with a gas can. "This is the last of it. Ought to get us out there and then to the mainland for a refill. Grab the empties from the clearing by the trailer and let's move out."

"What if we get shot at again?" Trufante moaned.

"I'll take care of that." Mac took the stairs to the house two at a time and opened the screen door. He couldn't help but notice how much the passive solar design had helped cool the house off. He walked into the bedroom and went to the closet, relieved when his hand grasped the warm steel of the gun barrel.

He pulled out the 410 shotgun. The chamber was empty and he had a moment of panic before he found the box of shells on the shelf. Pistol grip in one hand and ammunition in the other, he left the house and went down the stairs. It wasn't an AK or even a rifle, but the sound of a shotgun chambering its load was often as effective as a warning shot.

"Whatcha gonna do with the snake charmer? Damn thing's only good for shooting critters."

"It's more than we had a minute ago." He sat on the bottom step and loaded five shells in the chamber, then cocked the gun. "The bark's worse than the bite, that's for sure, but it's what we've got."

They walked together to the beach, Mac with the gun and

Trufante with the gas can. When they reached the boat, Trufante stowed the can and went to the small clearing to retrieve the empties there. Mac climbed over the gunwale and set the shotgun beside the driver's seat before starting the engine.

He had to admit he was happy with the way the motor sounded as he pushed the throttle slightly to ensure there were no hitches. Whoever was at the island was dangerous, and he needed to have enough confidence in the boat to get him out of there fast if things went bad.

Just then, Trufante handed four empty cans over and hopped in the boat. Mac looked at him as he secured the cans to the boat with a bungee cord and wondered how drunk he was. Not that he was much good in a fight anyway, but at least he could take orders if he was sober.

Trufante finished tying down the cans, sat in the other seat, and put his feet up on the dash. Mac reversed the boat out of the narrow channel, wishing it had twin outboards instead of the single. Two motors would have allowed him to put one in forward and the other in reverse, turning the boat on its center line. With only the single motor, he had to use the forward momentum of the boat to make a turn.

A hundred yards out he spun the wheel and waited for the boat to come perpendicular to the channel, then pushed down on the throttle and took off into the night.

* * *

Mel looked at the boat in the slip, wondering how much water the hull drew. She was probably the only person to evaluate the sleek cruiser by its draft. Everyone else admired its lines and expensive appointments. Not worried about the comfort the boat would provide, she was more worried about taking it into the backcountry. She moved to the stern of the thirty-something-foot vessel and looked in the water.

"Sweetie, no worries. She draws a smidgen less than two

feet. Better than most of these boats." Marvin waved his arms at the other boats moored in the marina, expensive outboards hanging from their transoms. "Twin drive and pretty fast."

Mel looked up, relieved. The shallowest flat they would have to cross was over three feet at low tide, and with the moon the way it looked, low tide was going to be pretty low tonight. But with an extra foot under the keel, they might be fine. It would be up to her to navigate the treacherous waters and make sure of that.

"Got a chart plotter?"

"Yes, and a blender. Ready for anything."

Mel hopped the short gap between the boat and the dock, landing easily on the clean fiberglass. She went to the helm and looked at the electronics. Satisfied, she turned to Marvin. "She'll do."

"Sweetie, she'll more than do." He went forward and untied the dock line, tossing it onto the bow, then went to the stern and released the line there. With a hop he was on the boat, key in hand. "I guess you ought to drive. I can barely get out of here in daylight."

Mel already had the engines started and waited for the gauges to come up. Once the engine had warmed, she pulled forward from the slip into the channel leading to the Gulf of Mexico. She held course close to the red markers—shining in the moonlight—on her port side, knowing the channel was deeper here. As soon as they passed the last marker, she pushed the throttles down.

"OK. We've got an hour and a bit. Let's hear what's going on with you."

* * *

The moon provided the perfect amount of light for Mac to navigate the dangerous waters at night. He kept the running lights on as he crossed the flats and entered Harbor Channel, figuring that with the light of the moon, the boat would be visible anyway. No reason to attract attention running dark like they were doing something wrong.

There was a faster, more direct way than backtracking to the channel, but at night, the slightest mistake would ground them. He saw the lighted pile marking the deeper water and turned west just short of it. Now on the outside of the chain of barrier islands, he got the boat up on plane and quickly covered the four miles to the Sawyer Keys. Ten minutes later, the outline of the mangrove lined shore came into view. He cut the running lights and slowed the boat.

He kept the boat a quarter mile offshore as he passed the entrance. He had intimate knowledge of many of the small keys in this area, but had never been interested in Sawyer, mainly because of the area's status as a Wildlife Management Area. There were plenty of other productive fishing and lobster grounds around, and he had no reason to be anywhere near a managed area, although that just added to the irony of Trufante getting caught here.

He had found a chart in Wood's living room and studied the island earlier, committing the shape, water depth, and landmarks to memory. The Sawyer Keys were exactly that—a cluster of mangrove-covered islands with a small lagoon and a tidal creek.

Looking at the cluster of islands from a bird's eye view on the chart, he'd seen where he had entered the concealed creek and where the building was. That approach was too dangerous, as was the more open entry from the shallow lagoon. He had passed by the larger Key several times and noticed a narrow beach on the seaward side of the island, and after seeing it on the chart, he felt comfortable that they could make landfall there and bushwhack through the mangroves to the other side of the island.

It wouldn't be pleasant, but he had no doubt they would be unobserved.

He took the boat past the island, headed inshore, and approached the islands by the unmarked Johnston Key Channel. The beach came into view and he slowed the boat further.

"Hey, toss the anchor," he said quietly.

"What you mean toss the anchor? Why don't you take her up on the beach?" Trufante whined.

Mac had no patience to negotiate; remembering the chart and knowing how low the tide would be later, he realized he wouldn't be able to plow through the sandy bottom to get out of there. It was out here, in the deeper water, or nothing.

He pulled back on the throttles, left the wheel, and went forward to open the hatch on the bow and take out the small anchor. It looked more like a dingy anchor, too light for the weight of this boat and he felt no better as he pulled out only eight feet of chain with it. Rental boats were famous for skimping on ground hardware, knowing that many customers would fight the charges when they lost the anchor and line. The waves rocked the light boat and he was thrown off balance as he held the chain in one hand and the hook in the other. It would have to do.

The anchor splashed as he dropped it into the six-foot-deep water and looked back at Trufante, who must have sensed Mac's anger and had gone to the wheel. Trufante pulled the throttle and the transmission clicked into reverse. Mac fed out the rode while Trufante backed down the boat. The current was with them, and the boat drifted closer to the island until it came to a quick stop as Mac tied off the line to a cleat. He had set much of the line out, hoping the extra scope would compensate for the small anchor and lack of chain.

He was over the side and into the waist-deep water, holding the shotgun over his head and a flashlight in his teeth, a moment later. He waited for Trufante, who joined him with a machete held over his head. They waded the one hundred feet to the beach and exited the water. There, Mac looked at the moon to get his bearings and motioned for Trufante to start hacking a trail through the brush as he held the light from behind. They waded through muck and swatted mosquitos for an hour as they slowly cut their way through the brush until they saw a small light through the branches.

Mac leaned toward Trufante and whispered, "Got to be quieter from here on out. I got it."

He took the machete and started slashing at the branches, his blistered hands stinging. He wondered if the rum had made Trufante's numb, since the other man hadn't said anything about it. They were getting scraped and bitten but moved faster now, as he cut as narrow a trail possible for them to get by.

Minutes later, they reached the end of the brush and stared at the back of the house ten feet away. The house was dark, with the exception of one window, where a light showed. Mac stepped out of the brush, hunched over, and ran for the house. Trufante was on his heels and they moved along the building, away from the light. They circumnavigated the structure and relaxed slightly when he noticed the boat was gone.

The house appeared to be empty, and he made his way to the lit window and nodded to Trufante, who at six foot five could easily see inside.

"Son of a bitch. There's some flesh in there."

"What are you talking about?" Mac inched closer to look in. He didn't have the vantage point of the Cajun, but he could clearly see three women lounging on cushions.

"Hot damn. I got to meet these ladies," Trufante mumbled, staring.

Mac started to pull him away when they heard a scream from the room. "Now you've done it."

Three faces stared back at him, one girl banging on the glass. It appeared they were trying to get his attention. One of the girls made a motion with her hands that looked like she wanted him to go around and unlock the door.

Mac knew the boat was gone, and was hoping the house was empty except for the women. He paused before he moved, trying to figure out if the women would be any benefit to him. In the end, although they might be trouble, he decided to see if they knew anything that could help him.

His mind made up, he headed for the front, Trufante following like a dog.

Chapter 15

The man watched the lights from shore with trepidation as the boat closed on the coast. It certainly wasn't America, he thought, as he waited for the boat to deliver him. The US coast was lit up like a Christmas tree, while here the lights were sparse and intermittent—a sure sign of the difference in economies and culture.

"You're coming back in two days, yes?" he asked the driver.

"I do what they tell me to do," Jay responded.

Both men scanned the horizon for the boat they were to meet. The GPS beeped, signaling that they had reached the waypoint assigned for the exchange.

"They better show soon, or you'll be swimming. This moon is too bright to be sitting here."

The man looked around. The driver was right—even without running lights, they were too visible. "Give them a few minutes."

"You must be picking up something special for them to order me out on a full moon," Jay said.

The man ignored him and kept scanning the water. Mariel was just west of Havana, and was a smaller town made famous for the stream of criminals Castro had sent North in 1980. In all, 125,000 Cubans, many from jails and mental health institutions, had been released here to find their way to America. Most on overcrowded rafts. He had been one of those men, and despite the thirty-plus years, could still recall the ordeal. His anxiety increased as he waited and he thought about the man he was to bring to freedom … and the riches. Baseball was huge in Cuba, and the small island produced many major league prospects.

But the regime refused to allow them to leave the country except for international competitions, where they were closely watched.

For several years now, he had been smuggling players to the United States to play. It was fairly easy to find the players. With the right equipment, which his cousin had access to, he could hear and see Cuban radio and television in the Southern states. And with the proliferation of the internet, there was plenty of information.

But each mission was getting more dangerous. Norm tried to focus on the lesser known up and coming players to attract less attention when they went missing, but it was not a big country, and he suspected the government had taken note. Even with the extractions spaced months apart, he felt it was only a matter of time before he was caught.

The regime, more worried about saving face than saving their country, took the loss of the half-dozen players now playing in America as a major blow, and were sure to devote resources to stop it.

"There." He pointed. The wake of a boat was visible in the moonlight as it ran fast toward them.

Jay grabbed a pair of binoculars sitting on the dashboard and focused on the boat. "Lucky bastard. It's them," he said as a light flashed twice from the bow. "I was liking the idea of watching you swim."

The man ignored him and went to the cargo. He started to undo the lashings holding the tarp in place, wanting to make this exchange as quickly as possible. The sooner he could get away from the gringo, the better. "What's this?"

Jay turned. "Underwater scooter and snorkel gear. That's

how you're coming out."

He turned and looked again at the cylinder with two handles and a small propeller. Hiding this contraption would be difficult, but he understood it would be safer to swim out rather than boarding a boat for the exchange. Even at night, there were always people watching, ready to report any suspicious activity to the regime.

Arriving by boat was safer. His clothes blended with the other men, and it was doubtful any watchers would remember how many men had left on any particular boat. His thoughts were broken when the other boat pulled alongside.

Jay spoke in Spanish to the driver, whose crew was busy tying lines to the bow and stern, securing the hulls together with fenders separating them in the three-foot waves. The boats drifted with the current as the exchange was made, and he was the last piece of cargo to board the older boat. A ball cap pulled low over his brow to hide his face, he went to the transom and leaned against it, waiting as the lines were freed and the driver pushed down the throttles and headed for the harbor.

* * *

Mac entered the house with the shotgun extended in front of him and Trufante trailing behind with the flashlight and machete. Ignoring the banging on the door where the women were held, they checked the house thoroughly before moving to the room with the women. A slide bolt had been installed on the exterior of the door, to prevent the occupants from leaving, and Mac hesitated before he unlocked it, knowing this was going to complicate things. In the end, he was unable to leave the women captive.

The bolt slid open and he turned the doorknob, entering the room with Trufante breathing on his neck. The women were clustered in a corner, clearly afraid.

Trufante slid past him. "Y'all are good now. Old Tru's going to take care of you." He went toward the women, but they tightened their grasp on each other.

"Back away," Mac warned him. "We don't have much time," he addressed the girls. "One of you tell me what's going on here, and we'll try to help."

"Damn right we'll help," Trufante piped in.

Mac glared at him and waited for the women, who were now whispering to each other. Finally one moved to the front.

"Please. We are being held here. Can you just get us off this island? We promise we won't be any trouble." She tried to smile, but he could see the fear in her eyes.

"Come on, Mac," Trufante pleaded. "We gotta help them."

Mac was about to snap at him to rearrange his priorities, but he knew he couldn't leave them here. Whatever was going on was wrong, and if he had the ability to help, he knew he would. There was also the chance that he might get lucky and get some information out of them that could help his case. Maybe he could use them for leverage.

"Go pull the boat around. We can't take them into the brush like this." He stared at them—barefoot and dressed in skimpy silk robes.

"On it." Trufante ran from the room.

"We're going to get you out of here. Do you have anything more substantial to wear?"

All three shook their heads.

"Get what you can carry and head out to the dock. I'm going to have a look around."

He left the room and went into the bedroom down the hall. There was no need for subterfuge now; the owner would know someone had been here once he saw the girls gone. So he pulled the drawers from the dresser and tossed their contents on the floor. Empty handed he left the bedroom and went toward two French doors further down the hall. But they were locked.

Without a second thought, he slammed the pistol grip of the

shotgun down onto the levers and smashed the lock. He pushed the door open and entered a small office.

The desk top was bare, so he moved to the drawers, searching them one at a time. Finding nothing of value, he turned to the credenza behind him. The countertop had mementos of a life overseas, with several framed pictures. He glanced at the memorabilia, trying to find anything that would tie the man to his situation. One picture showed him in front of a statue in what looked like a government building, side by side with an older man in a suit.

The only clue so far, he grabbed it. Trufante should be back any minute, and he wanted to get out of there before the occupant returned.

He traced his way through the dark house, not wanting to turn on any lights, and found the front door. Outside, he followed the patio to the dock and stood by the girls in silence as they listened for the sound of an approaching boat.

* * *

The old wooden fishing boat had passed through the inlet and entered a small bay, staying close to the decrepit industrial pier on his right. The driver headed toward the lights of the town, staying in the deeper water before turning toward a dark area. There he'd stopped the boat a few hundred yards from shore and told the man it was time. He sat on the gunwale and spun toward the water as the other men on the boat handed him the scooter, mask, and fins. Carefully he slid into the water, hoping it would be solid ground below his feet and not muck. Attaching the lanyard from the scooter to his wrist and gathering the two sets of snorkeling gear in the other hand, he started wading through the knee-deep water toward land.

He reached the mangrove-lined shore near the brightly lit ball field and searched for a place to make landfall. A gap in the mangroves was to his right, and he headed toward the small spit of sand. Once there, he looked for a place to hide his gear. He found an old tree with its roots exposed by years of storms and erosion, mostly above the water mark, and slipped the gear into the opening in the roots. Then he went back to the tideline and gathered an armful of seaweed and leaves, brought them back to the tree, and concealed the scooter with them.

Satisfied the gear was secure, he pushed through the brush toward the lights and sound of a crowd. The branches opened into a large clearing he knew to be the town's baseball field, and he walked under the bleachers. Waiting there was another man, who shook his hand. Then the two men went up into the bleachers.

They sat and watched the game, making sure to leave several rows between them and the other spectators.

"That's him," the second man said. "He's been in for a couple of innings now."

"Got good stuff. Looks to be throwing in the 80s."

"Only on a day's rest, too. You let that boy get three or four days and he'll be in the high 90s."

The man relaxed and smiled as he watched the boy named Armando Cruz finish the inning. Maybe Norm was right on this one.

* * *

Mel guided them through the narrow channel, eased off the throttles, and allowed the boat to come to a stop at the pier. There was no sign of life, but she hadn't expected any. Mac was probably up at the house, and more than likely asleep.

"Do you have a light?" she asked.

Marvin reached into his pocket and took out a lighter.

"Um, no. A flashlight."

"Oh. Of course, there's probably one below." He went into the cabin.

The mosquitos had found them, and a small cloud had formed; probably attracted by his cologne, she thought as she waited for him. A minute later he emerged with a Maglite and a can of insect repellent.

"Bug bites are bad for the complexion." He sprayed himself liberally and handed the can to her.

She took it and hesitated before spraying herself, loathing the smell and feel of the chemicals. But when a mass of bugs swarmed her head, she applied the repellent. Then, flashlight in hand, she slid off into the water—only ankle deep at the bow, now with the tide at its low point—and waded toward the beach. She turned to make sure Marvin was following, but he sat in a deck chair.

"You coming?"

"No, sweetie. You can do your nature hike, visit the boyfriend thing. I'll be fine here."

She turned and noticed that the trail was freshly trimmed as she went toward the clearing. The house appeared, dark in the moonlight, and she went up the stairs. The door was closed, which she thought unusual in the heat. Normally the screen door would be the only obstacle to entry. She opened the door and reached for the light switch to turn on the lights, but nothing happened.

"Mac!" she called out as she went to the bedroom, shining the flashlight in front of her. The room was empty as well; the bed not slept in. Something out of place grabbed her attention and she went to the nightstand by the bed and looked at the thumb drive and felt bag. It certainly wasn't her father's and she doubted Mac knew what to do with it. Curious, she put them in her pocket, left the room and went through the living room toward the front door. Standing on the porch, she shone the light at the shed and surrounding areas. Nothing was out of place, except a pile of gear near the shed door.

Maybe he had gone fishing; full moons were often productive at night on the flats. With nothing to do but wait, she climbed the stairs to escape the bugs and sat in one of the deck chairs. She was anxious about Mac, but knew he could take care of himself.

For the first time since Marvin had gone through the financials, she had the time to digest what he had discovered. She needed to figure out how Cayenne's financial shenanigans could be used to help Mac. Leverage was the answer, call it blackmail if you wanted, but she could agree to keep quiet about the books if she would testify in Mac's favor. But, she was not sure the woman would cooperate. Getting her to understand logic was like teaching a dog to meow.

Unable to sit still, she got up, went down the stairs, and headed back toward the water. She was standing on the beach when she saw the running lights from a small boat approaching.

Chapter 16

Mel did a double take as the boat approached. It looked like a ghost from the past, the hull showing a makeshift plywood patch in the moonlight,. She knew it had been sitting on the far side of the island since beaching and injuring her father several years ago, but who had fixed it? And why? She recognized Trufante first; hard to miss, between his height and his grin. As the boat closed, she could see Mac at the wheel and several other figures huddled behind the men.

Her smile turned to anger as the boat drew close enough to see that they were women.

Marvin appeared with two fenders in hand, which he placed over the side as Mac coasted toward the larger boat and Trufante tied the two boats together. Mel yelled from the beach.

He looked dumbfounded.

"Girls! Two days and you two go pick up women. And to think I was worried about you. No calls. No texts. Now this!" She turned to Marvin. "Untie them. We're out of here."

Mac jumped over the side and ran through the water toward the beach. "We just saved these girls. They were captives at a house on Sawyer."

"Sure. And Tru looks like the cat that just caught the mouse. Come on, Mac. You expect me to believe that?"

"Tell her, Tru."

She pushed away from Mac, stomped through the shallow water toward Marvin's boat, and climbed onto the swim platform. With a look of disgust, she pushed the small door cut into the transom open and entered the cockpit.

"Start this thing and let's go," she said as she went for the lines, untying and casting them in the water.

Marvin finally stopped staring and started the engines, put the boat in reverse, and backed away. Before she could get to the wheel, though, the boat grounded. She crossed the deck in two strides and pushed Marvin away from the helm. Stepping into his place, she pulled back on the throttles, gently at first. Then, when the boat didn't move, she shoved them back to their stops.

Frustrated, she looked behind the boat as the propeller shot sand and muck into the cut. Finally, the boat moved slightly. With her teeth gritted and a look of determination, she held her hand steady on the controls as the boat slid off the sandbar.

She almost waited too long, as the boat jerked backwards with enough momentum to ground the stern on the other side of the cut, but she was able to shift the boat into forward, bypassing neutral and causing a bang in the transmission. Free and in the center of the channel, she sped away without looking back.

* * *

Mac watched in horror as the boat moved into open water. Instead of taking action and stopping her to explain about the house and the girls, he had stood speechless and let her go. In truth, he knew from experience that there was no stopping her. When Mel made up her mind it was a done deal.

"Get them out of the boat and back to the house. I'm going after her," he yelled and helped the last girl over the side. With a shot of anger and adrenaline surging through him, he vaulted the gunwale and went for the controls.

The larger boat was still visible in the distance, the moon

reflecting off the polished chrome, and he thought he had a good chance of catching them as he reversed the engine and waited for the boat's momentum to turn the hull. Finally it faced the exit to the channel, and he pushed down on the throttle.

The larger boat was much faster, and was distancing itself from him, but when he saw it turn west at the edge of the bank he knew they were heading toward Key West. They were up on plane, running on the outside of the barrier islands, and that was the most probable destination. Confused and upset about what happened, he continued to follow.

He was just past the Content Keys and approaching the Sawyer Keys, the white anchor light still visible in the distance, when he began to worry. He appeared to be closing the gap between the boats. Mel knew these waters well enough to run blind in a hurricane, and there was no reason for her to slow ... unless something was wrong.

Suddenly another boat appeared, its red and green running lights indicating a collision course with Mel's boat. He pushed down on the throttle in an attempt to reach the oncoming boat before the other craft, but his engine sputtered. He eased back on the throttle and the engine seemed to catch, but as soon as he asked it for more power it failed, and he was adrift. He went to the gas can and kicked it, knowing it was empty.

There was no way he'd be able to reach Mel in time to prevent the collision.

The tide was moving the boat away from the action now, so he made the only move he had available and went forward to throw the anchor. It caught in the sand, and he tied it off, then went to the stern to check whether there was any gas left in the tanks he'd had Trufante stow. Even a quart would get him back to Wood's Island.

But they were bone dry. Anything left had evaporated in the heat. When he looked up again, he couldn't see the white light anymore. Unless something catastrophic had happened, Mel was further west and out of sight.

* * *

Cayenne was drunk. She was also incensed at the way Mel had treated her. She could have any man she wanted—gay or not— and how dare Mel say otherwise? As she wandered down Duval Street, weaving her way through the crowd, with one goal in mind … well two, actually, but she could only wrap her head around sex. Her mounting money problems would have to wait.

She'd had her eye on the man that had captained the boat she'd chartered the other day for a while, and after seeing him tonight in the oyster bar, her hormones were in the red zone. Hoping he was still there, she hailed a rickshaw powered by a bicycle rider and stumbled into the seat. The driver took off through the traffic, thick with cars, scooters, golf carts, and bicycles, jerking left and right to avoid the people overflowing into the streets. Traffic thinned as they turned off Duvall, and five minutes later the driver pulled up at the courtyard in front of the oyster bar. She fished in her purse to pay the driver and, finding only twenties, tossed one at him.

The bar was still full, although the restaurant had cleared out. At first she didn't see him, but a couple moved out of the way and there he was. She inhaled deeply, trying to steady herself, and went after him, pushing her boobs forward through the crowd.

"Hey, sailor. Come here often?" She didn't care how lame the pick-up line was. The guy was fixated on her chest.

He stuttered, "Miss Cannady."

She pushed up against him. "Don't you 'Miss Cannady' me. My special friends call me Cay. And tonight I think you're going to be one of those friends. Now get me a drink."

* * *

Mel ran a safe distance from the boundary islands, reaching Key West an hour later, the boat she had nearly collided with by the Sawyer Keys long forgotten. She figured there was a good chance the driver had the auto-pilot on, or just wasn't paying attention. As dangerous as the backcountry could be, once you were past the chain of islands, the water became deep enough to travel without worry, and there was little traffic at night and it wasn't unusual to have the autopilot on.

She slowed as they reached the first marker leading to the marina and pulled back to idle speed after the wake caught the boat, pushing it forward. Minutes later she skillfully backed into Marvin's slip and cut the engines as he tied off the boat.

The ride had been exhilarating. Running at night always got the blood pumping. Her concentration had been so intense that she barely thought about Mac the entire ride back. Now her anger returned in force. She jumped onto the dock looking for something to take her tension out on.

"I'm going in for a drink," she called to Marvin over her shoulder. "You coming?"

"Sweetie. After that ride? You bet." He followed her into the bar.

Mel opened the door and had started across the threshold when she saw Cayenne with the boat captain. That was the last thing she needed. Hoping the redheaded witch hadn't seen her, she started backing out the door.

* * *

Mac stood in the bow powerless to act. A mullet jumping in front of the boat distracted him. Except for everything in his life going wrong, it would have been sweet to be anchored out here with the full moon casting light on the small waves, a cast net on his shoulder, ready to toss at the unsuspecting fish.

But the illusion shattered as he saw the lights coming toward him change, indicating that they were making a hard right turn into the concealed inlet. He had a moment of panic before the boat turned that there might be a confrontation, but he realized now that he posed no threat, even if the other driver had seen him. It was not uncommon to fish—even in these unmarked waters—on a full moon. The captain of the other boat had probably taken Mac for a fisherman.

That didn't alter his problem: stuck in the middle of nowhere, out of gas. After trying the VHF radio and finding it non-functional, he went back to the bow and stared into the dark water, thinking about his options. He could always hang out until daylight, when there was a chance a boat would spot him. But the wind was starting to pick up again and that would keep most of the boats in port. His other option was to swim for it, and the desire to find out what the man in the other boat was up to made his decision for him. Once he reached land, he would at least have more options than here in the water.

Without a second thought, he slid into the neck-deep water. The tide was pulling away from land now, but he was a strong swimmer and only had a couple hundred yards to cover. He settled into a side stroke, using a lone tree, taller than the surrounding mangroves, as an easy landmark. Fifteen minutes later he stood and waded the remaining fifty feet to land … or what he hoped would be land.

Sometimes mangroves didn't indicate shores at all, but places where the long-rooted trees managed to grow in deeper, fresher water.

He started to work his way through the tangle of roots, wary for the predators they housed. Spiders dropped onto his head from above and he felt crabs nipping at his bare feet. Slowly the water became shallower, though, and soon he was on dry land.

He wiped back his sweat-drenched hair to rid it of insects and continued in the direction he thought the house lay. From the charts he had studied and the previous trip, he knew he was on a smaller key separated from the larger island with the house by a small tidal creek. This gave him some security, as he knew he was alone and would not have to worry about being observed until he crossed the creek.

His thought was to steal either some gas or one of the boats to get back to Wood's, and if he could escape unobserved, grab the rental boat and tow it behind. That would give Trufante transportation to get himself and the girls to land and—more importantly—away from him.

Second, he would have a boat to get to Key West and straighten things out with Mel.

The mangroves thinned as he reached the center of the island, allowing him to move quickly toward the sandy shore of the creek. Across the way, he could make out several lights on in the house, and realized his escape might be more difficult than he originally thought; with the girls gone whoever was there would have realized that an intruder had been there. He would have to be extra cautious to avoid the man.

He crouched down on the beach and slid into the water, listening for any unusual sound. Totally exposed, he realized the best thing he could do was to get across. Two breaths later he submerged and started stroking toward the other bank, reaching it without incident. He pulled himself onto the sand and crawled to the mangroves twenty feet from the beach.

The house was about one hundred yards away and he heard a lone voice—probably a one-sided phone conversation. He made his way toward the boats, staying close to the mangroves and keeping as much distance between himself and the house as possible. He reached a point where he had to make a decision; either swim across to the boats or stay on land to reach the exposed docks.

Already soaking wet, he decided to swim across. Silently he entered the water and side stroked to the far bank. Now, with the mangroves shielding him, he worked his way toward the boats.

His first thought was to take the larger craft. The forty-foot-plus hull with its three 275-hp outboards gleamed in the moonlight, but he thought the smaller center console would serve his purposes better. It would also probably have more fuel than the larger boat, which had just returned. He could still hear the man in the house as he reached the boat and climbed the swim ladder. On deck, he stayed below the gunwales as he crawled to the helm.

There was no key in the ignition, but he hadn't really expected to find one. And it didn't matter for the short term. He planned to paddle out of the small cove before starting the engine.

But before he could do anything, a door slammed and the man came outside, a flashlight in his hand. Mac hit the deck.

Chapter 17

Mel eased her way out the door and walked past the bicycle stand to a statue of an anchor in the square.

"Sweetie, what's the matter? I thought you wanted a drink."

"Didn't you see her in there hitting on that guy? All sloppy and brushing her tits against him."

"Now, now. We can go somewhere else," Marvin said.

Mel looked around. "No, that's OK. I think I'll take a quick run back to the house and try and clear my head. Things just haven't gone well for me today, and I need some time to digest all this." She turned to go.

"Well, you know where to find me if you need me." He hugged her and kissed a tear from her cheek.

She hadn't meant to cry, but his touch released the pent-up emotions of the past few hours. Furious with Mac and maddened by Cayenne's ineptitude, larceny, or a combination of both, she just needed to run.

Her head started to clear as she accelerated after holding back for the first few blocks. Rather than trusting the assortment of island vehicles to see her, she used them as an obstacle course, swerving between the sidewalk and street. The challenge helped her to focus, and she fell into a rhythm as she reached Truman and turned left. Cayenne's house was only blocks away, but she was feeling good and continued toward the beach, where the sea breeze greeted her and she headed towards the waterline.

She ran along the high tide mark where the sand was firmer until she slowed by a deserted section of beach near a slaving memorial. She started walking toward the water, took off her shoes, and followed the line where the water hit the sand.

Her immediate anger with Mac had faded, and she knew she needed to consider that there might be another side to the story. Of course, with Trufante involved anything could have happened, but picking up girls and bringing them back to Wood's was out of character for Mac. She knew him to be a loner at heart, and he stayed away from trouble.

It was Trufante who usually brought it.

Coral Gardens—or The silicone slush fund, as she was now calling it—was a different matter. The woman was corrupt, and she didn't want to go back to the house—or to work. But there were still questions to be answered, and the only way to help Mac was to suck it up and follow through. With a plan forming in her mind, she went back to the road, put her shoes back on, and started walking toward the house.

When she turned onto the street, she couldn't help but notice that the lights were on and a strange truck was in the driveway. Not wanting to burst in on something, she approached the house slowly and climbed the porch steps, not sure if she was going in or not. Two people were visible as she looked in the window—Cayenne, with her top off, and the captain.

She could hear them talking, but couldn't make out the words from where she stood, so without thinking she moved closer and stood by the side of the window.

"What do you mean you're going to pay me with lobster?" the captain snapped.

"Honey, it'll be worth your while. I just gotta get out there one more time. I'm telling you, if we haul in anything close to what we got the other day, you'll have a pocket full of money."

"That's called poaching, and I could lose my license if we

get caught," the man responded.

Cayenne brushed against him. "Sometimes you got to stick it out there if you want the reward."

Mel sat down on the deck underneath the window and tried to get the vision of Cayenne out of her head, but still process what she had heard. This only further confirmed everything she had suspected. She had the motive, that was for sure, *and* the opportunity; the only thing she needed was an idiot with a boat to do the work ... and Trufante fit that bill perfectly. If she could just get her to confess it would clear Mac, but confronting her was not likely to get results. Cayenne thought she was above the law and would laugh at Mel's accusations. What she needed was proof. All the better if she could ruin the witch and help Mac in the process.

The house was quiet now, and she crawled onto her knees to look in the window. The room was empty, the only sign of its previous inhabitants Cayenne's top and bra lying on the floor. She sat back down and started thinking, wanting to kill a few minutes before she entered the house.

* * *

Mac hugged the deck of the boat, trying to stay out of sight as the man approached. He could hear footsteps on the dock coming closer, but they stopped and he held his breath. Then he heard movement again, but it seemed like the guy was moving away.

He breathed, but stayed where he was. The minutes dragged on until he was sure he was alone. Slowly he raised his body to a sitting position and peered over the gunwale.

A light hit him in the face and he shrunk, but it was too late.

"You think you're dealing with an amateur?"

Mac could hear the action of the gun as the man cocked it.

"Don't worry. You don't need to answer now. That will all come in time. Now get on your feet and step onto the dock with your arms over your head. And, for what it's worth, there is no one within a mile of here, so if you try anything I'll plug you and leave you in the cove for the crabs."

Mac looked around the boat for any option, but found none. He raised himself to his full height and stepped over the side of the boat, placing one foot on the wooden dock and then the other.

"Good. I see you've already been swimming. Water's nice, huh?"

Mac nodded.

"By the way, that's how I found you. The wet spot on the boat's side where you climbed over. Now you're going to meet a friend of mine." He motioned the gun for Mac to move toward him.

Mac followed along. He knew he would have to endure whatever the man had planned until an opportunity presented itself to escape. He almost took the chance of pushing him off the dock as he passed by, but the man was equal height and weight, and Mac suspected he knew how to use his body. In front of the man now, he walked off the dock and onto the patio.

"This way." The man motioned toward an enclosure in the water.

Mac walked to the edge of the patio and looked at what appeared to be an ordinary storage cage that fishermen used to keep live bait overnight, but on a much bigger scale. The enclosure was at least ten feet square, with the wire standing two feet above the water and a single strand of barbed wire on top. The posts were spaced close enough to ensure the wire stayed tight. Once in, Mac knew there would be no easy escape.

The man walked ahead of him and opened a small gate cut into the side adjacent to the shore. He pointed the gun at Mac and signaled his intent.

Mac walked slowly toward the opening, looking around for any opportunity to escape, but there was nothing. Desperate now, he pulled an arm forward to elbow the man in the ribs, but a hard kick in the back took him by surprise, forcing him into the water. His head went below and there was an instant of panic before his feet hit the sandy bottom and he pushed up. Just as he recovered, the gate was closed and he heard the hasp of a padlock snap shut. He tried to stand on the bottom, but his mouth remained submerged, forcing him to tread water. The man stood there in front of him with a grin on his face.

"Don't worry." He picked up a long foam swim noodle. "You can have this if you answer some questions for me. And believe me, you're going to need it. You see there's something in there that should be introducing itself to you any second now." He paused.

Mac didn't know what to make of what he said and continued to tread water. Then out of nowhere, he felt stinging as something circled around and through his legs.

"Ah, I see by the look on your face that you have met my friend. Now if you want this—" He held out the noodle. "—You can start by telling me where the girls are."

"What girls? I just ran out of gas out there," he played dumb.

"Don't give me that line. You were prowling around in here with some other guy earlier. I shot at your ass."

"Just got lost, is all," Mac pleaded. "A buddy gave me some numbers for a good lobster hole."

"I don't believe in coincidences, and seeing you twice in one day is a large one. Now, start talking."

Mac was getting tired from treading water. Whatever was in the water was still circling him, and a tingling sensation went through his body whenever it touched him. He was just about to reach for the fencing to hold himself when he saw a large mosquito run into the wire. A bright blue light sparked, and with a zap the bug fell into he water.

The pen was electrified. He moved back toward the center, away from the fence. It must be an eel he thought, the creature must be channeling the current. The man must have caught his look. "I see you know my little secret now. But here's the thing." He went toward a table and picked up a box. "I can turn up the voltage as well. Right now it's probably a little tingling, but another few volts and you'll be singing."

Mac thought about his predicament. There was no way out as long as the man was there. "OK. I'm looking for a poacher that set me up. The girls are with my buddy. You let me go and I'll bring them back."

"What do you take me for?" The man sat with the box on his lap and turned up the dial. The tingling was now stinging. "I don't give a crap about the girls. They're just flesh, and I was getting bored with them anyway. Plenty more where that came from. The thing is, you trespassed on my very private piece of property, and now I'm going to have to get rid of you. But first you're going to take me to your friend."

Mac knew he was safe as long as Trufante remained at large. The man had no idea what they knew and had no way of finding Trufante without his help. "OK. I'll take you to him."

"I'm a little tired. Been a long day." The guy got up and set the box on the chair. "Enjoy yourself overnight." He tossed the noodle to Mac. "The more you move, the more excited he gets." And he walked away.

Mac was alone now, his arms hanging over the foam. It kept him afloat and the eel had stopped harassing him as long as he remained still. He looked around for any means of escape, trying desperately to find a way out of the pen.

Somehow, this man and his island held his get-out-of-jail-free card; he just needed to figure it out. Like the man had said, he didn't believe in coincidences either, and this guy was some bad stuff, be it women, drugs, or smuggling it didn't matter. It stood to reason that he had taken whatever those crates were that Commando had on his boat, as well as women, and who knows what else. There had to be an answer here, he just had to escape the pen.

Chapter 18

Mel was up at dawn, knowing that it would probably be several hours before Cayenne made an appearance. She dug the tax returns from her backpack and went to her office, where she ran copies and replaced the originals. Her heart was pounding and she was still not clear on what to do and how to deal with Mac, so she did what worked for her and put on her running shoes, slipped her phone into an armband, placed the earbuds in, and headed out the door.

Not wanting to miss Cayenne, she decided on a sprint workout. After pacing off one hundred yards on the street, she started a half-effort sprint back to the house. After warming up with some squats and pushups, she started running all-out efforts, walking back to the house to get her heart rate down after each one. Just about to start her ninth round, she heard someone outside the house and ducked behind the truck. Looking up, she saw that Cayenne and the captain were about to leave.

She crossed to the neighbor's driveway, staying tight to the hibiscus bushes and hoping they would shield her from the duo. Now only a few feet from them, but hidden by the shrubs, she could hear them clearly.

"You're sure this is cool?" the man asked.

"Honey, I'm not going to risk all this," Cayenne said. "We go out like the other days and have a look at the coral, but we make a slight detour and fill a couple of coolers with lobsters. You've taken me out there often enough that if anyone is watching, they've already seen you and won't suspect anything.

"A half-hour, that's all. And I'm staying on board. You're going to have to dive yourself."

Mel heard the doors close and the engine start. She stayed where she was until the truck had pulled out of the driveway. Her phone was out of the elastic armband before they had turned the corner.

"Marvin. Get up. We have to go back there now." She waited impatiently for him to gain his senses after obviously waking him.

"Sweetie, what time is it?" he murmured.

"It's time to get moving. Come on. I need you here. She's with that captain guy and they're heading back to the casitas. This is my chance to catch her red handed and clear Mac." She waited for a response, but none came. "Half-hour on the dock."

She hung up, crossed back onto Cayenne's property, and went into the house. A quick change of clothes from what little she had brought from Mac's and she was out the door and in the truck. Just being in Mac's truck made her think about him and regret the way she had handled things last night. She had information that could help and she needed to get to him quickly.

Invigorated from the sprints and ready to take action, she felt better than she had in months. The thought of watching Cayenne fall from whatever status she still had only added to her mood.

As she drove, she tried to plan her strategy for setting up Cayenne and clearing Mac. But as she started to think it through, she realized it wasn't as simple as it seemed. Calling Fish and Game or the Marine Patrol would only get Cayenne put in jail, and there wouldn't be any leverage to clear Mac in that case. No reason for her to *further* implicate herself, especially after her father would send a plane load of suits to bully the locals and represent her.

No, she needed to catch her red-handed and prove that the casitas were located inside her coral lease. Then she could offer some kind of deal to keep her out of jail. She had no idea how that was going to work, but she had a little time to think of something. The key was to catch her in the act.

The marina was busy when she pulled into the parking lot. Fishermen, divers, snorkelers, and sight seers were congregated on the docks, waiting for their charters. She pushed through a throng of middle-aged tourists and jumped down to the deck of Marvin's boat, where she pulled out her phone and checked the time of the call to Marvin. It had been forty minutes already, and she was getting anxious when the crowd parted and Marvin appeared.

She had the dock lines off before he was on the boat, and watched him sit on the dock before swinging his legs over and easing onto the deck. His hangover was evident, and after watching his unathletic entrance to the boat, she realized he was going to be of no use if things got ugly out there.

But he was all she had.

He went to the helm, inserted the key into the ignition, and clipped the dead man's key into its slot. The engines roared to life and he pulled out into the channel.

Mel was happy to let him drive—at least for now—so she could focus on figuring out how to corner Cayenne.

* * *

The man had spent the night in a small shack on the outskirts of town. He knew it was better to forego comfort and remain unseen. Mariel was a small town, and—typical of many Cuban villages—people neither moved in or out. The chances of running into someone that knew him were too high to risk. He climbed out of the cot and stretched his back. Between the boat ride and the old army cot, which looked like a remnant from the Spanish-American war, his body ached.

He went to the small kitchen, set a pot of water on the stove to boil for coffee, sat in one of the two older chairs, and waited. There was nothing he could do until his contact arrived but drink coffee. He reached for his pocket, instinctively looking for his cell phone, but realized he had left it in the States. It would be no use to him here.

Stashed under the shack was a locally purchased pre-paid phone that could access the internet. He would use GuerillaMail to send the message that all was ready for pick up. The anonymous mail server would send the message and within an hour scrub it from the server, so they couldn't be tracked.

The woman came in a half-hour and two cups of Cuban coffee later, and handed him a thin newspaper and a bag containing a pastry. She avoided his gaze and walked back out. He refilled his coffee and opened the paper. Usually filled with propaganda and sports, something on the front page caught his eye. He read the article with increasing interest and anxiety. The industrial pier he had passed on the way into the sound was scheduled to have Naval exercises starting tomorrow. Castro went all out on these occasions, taking his limited fleet and putting it in one place for the cameras to show the country that he still had power.

This was bad news, as it would force him to accelerate his extraction. The Cuban Navy, although far from its technologically advanced neighbor, still had enough machinery and manpower to cover the small bay. Once they started to arrive, his odds of getting out unseen were small. And waiting until the operation was over was out of the question. The way they scheduled things here, the Navy could be moving in for the winter.

He got up and went to the back door, where he peered out to see if anyone was watching and crept to the opening of the crawl space. Checking again to make sure he was unobserved, he pulled the access door off and slithered underneath the house. Moist sand and spider webs covered him as he crawled to the large girder that supported the floor joists. He reached his hand on top and moved it back and forth, looking for the bag. Finally he felt the plastic and pulled it out, stuffing the bag into his shirt.

Back in the kitchen, he pulled the phone out of the bag, inserted a SIM chip into it, and turned it on. The card had never been used and would be destroyed as soon as the message was sent. He went immediately to the web browser and entered the address for GuerillaMail. Hunched over the phone, he entered Norm's private email and punched in the message to move the extraction to sunset.

* * *

Mac had been shivering for hours when dawn finally broke, and he knew he was past the point of no return if he didn't get out of the trap soon. Although the tropical waters surrounding the Keys rarely dipped below eighty degrees, that was still cold enough to cause hypothermia; it just took a while. The eight hours that he'd been captive was already affecting his entire nervous system. He had been experiencing uncontrollable shivering and muscle cramps—symptoms that he was hypothermic. Without the foam noodle to support him and keep his upper body out of the water, he might be dead.

Now that it was light, he searched for any means of escape that he'd been unable to see last night. There was nothing in sight that he could reach, though, and he glanced down in the water. With the increasing light, the water was clear enough to see the bottom, and he could see the eel's head swaying in the current, its body hidden under a rock. It must have been at least five feet long, from the size of the head.

A door slammed and he turned to see the man coming toward him with two bottles of water in his hands. He tossed one toward Mac, and went to a freezer underneath the lanai, where he pulled out a fish carcass. He walked back to the pen and tossed it into the water.

"Gotta feed your friend there, we don't want him eating you while I'm gone. I gotta go run an errand. Try and save the Nationals' season, if you can believe it. You be a good boy now

133

and we'll have another chat later. Until then." He nodded at Mac and went toward the big boat.

Mac grabbed for the plastic bottle, barely able to grasp it before it sank, and tried to balance himself and open it. His fingers barely obeyed the command from his brain. The boat started, but he stayed focused on the task at hand, worried that he could not grip the cap. Finally he put it in his mouth and used his teeth as a vise to open the bottle. He spit out the cap and started to drink as he watched the boat move away.

Again he assessed his situation. The sun was rising now and the feel of its rays on his head brought some clarity back to his thoughts. He had to figure a way out and now.

The only tools at hand were the noodle and plastic bottle—both useless against the metal cage. The water level was rising, and only a foot of wire extended above the water, now. With the tide still incoming, he thought, this was the time to make whatever move he could. He leaned on the noodle and settled back to wait for high water.

When the tide crested, he would take the noodle to insulate and protect his hands and vault the fence. As he waited, the warmth of the sun quickly lulled him into a semi-conscious state.

* * *

Jay had to stop in Key West for gas—another annoying delay—but he had used almost three-quarters of his fuel on the last trip. Crossing the Gulfstream to reach Cuba took twice as much fuel, running into the 6-knot current as it did on the way back.

After filling the three tanks with one hundred gallons each, he headed back to the blue water to make the crossing. The wind was still up, but the weather was good at least, and crossing in the day was much safer than at night. He watched the tachometers and tuned each engine to 3800 rpms—a little slower than the previous trip, but more economical. Might as well save some dollars; the fill had cost him $1,800, and he didn't need to arrive before dusk.

The early extraction made this a one-way trip, and he'd had no time to organize any contraband for delivery. While he steered he calculated the fuel cost, deciding to add a surcharge onto his bill. The bean counters at the CIA would surely understand the economics of smuggling.

* * *

The man washed off in the old porcelain basin and wished he had another shirt. But at least with the dirty clothes and no deodorant, he would fit in perfectly. His contact had left several minutes ago, with instructions to deliver the player to the beach at 4pm. With six hours to kill, he slicked back his hair and left the shack.

The streets were quiet in the heat of the day, and he went unnoticed as he walked the dirt road, avoiding the main streets. Soon he reached a modest house, at least for the impoverished area, opened the short chain link gate, and followed the path to the door. He knocked and waited, a picture of her from several years ago in his head.

It was a risk—one he never would have taken if he weren't leaving later in the day—but seeing the woman was on his mind whenever he set foot on the island's soil. It was several years since he had waited on this stoop, and wondered what she would do.

His question was answered when the door opened and a man crowded the opening. He took one look at the figure and turned away.

"If you are looking for Maria, she does not want to see you," the man in the doorway said.

He kept walking, not wanting to show his face. He would have to be careful now, maybe just go to the beach and hide.

As he walked back to the beach, taking the most remote route, he started to glance over his shoulder. The man would certainly call the police. There was bound to be some kind of a reward for turning him in. This was the politics of Cuba.

Chapter 19

Something bumped the pen, waking Mac from his stupor. He looked up at the sun, now high in the sky, to try and gauge how long he had been out when the cage shook again. Around him, chunks of fish were floating in the water both inside and outside the cage. The last thing he remembered was the man tossing the carcass into the water before leaving.

The eel had been subdued during the night, possibly realizing the size of the man in the cage, but whatever the reason, the warm water had turned the frozen fish into chum that was now formed into a slick, floating out of the cove with the tide.

He suspected the bump was caused by one of the large bull sharks that roamed the flats, drawn in by the chum slick. But from his position, he was unable to see anything but his feet; the glare from the water hit his eyes as he tried to look for the culprit.

The cage shook again, and he had an idea. Suddenly awake, his adrenaline telling him this was his last chance, he studied the structure of the cage. In the daylight he could see the netting was made of PVC with strands of uninsulated wire, intertwined every foot or so to conduct electricity.

He saw a dorsal fin cut through the water and started to work his feet along the bottom until one of his toes snagged the fish carcass. The eel was far from his mind—probably hiding from the larger predator, not knowing it was safe inside the cage. He pinched two toes together and lifted his foot to waist level where he was able to grab hold of the fish and stick it in the space between two of the wires. There, he rubbed it back and forth against the mesh.

The fish started to disintegrate, and he hoped the shark would take the bait before it dissipated.

He rubbed the fish again, but his hand hit the wire and he jerked his had back from an electrical shock, releasing the fish to the bottom. It took several minutes to recover the carcass before he could start the process over.

This time the shark went for the fish, slamming into the enclosure between the two wires. It drove its head further into the space, touching both wires as Mac pulled the carcass from its reach.

Nothing happened. The shark's skin must be too dense for the current to penetrate it.

Mac pushed the fish forward, holding the carcass inches from the shark's nose, fully aware that it could easily tear through the netting, but it went for the bait and slid further between the wires.

He was out of room, pinned against the seawall as the shark came closer. It was inches from him when he pushed the fish against a wire and stuffed the carcass in its mouth. The fireworks started and sparks flew from the wires as the cage shorted and the shark stopped.

He wasn't sure if it was dead or stunned, and was not inclined to find out. With a section of the torn swim noodle in each hand to protect him from the wire, he hoisted himself onto the barbed wire and gained the seawall, where he lay motionless.

It took several minutes for him to recover his wits. He was still shivering, but the sun was warming him quickly. A look into the cage revealed the shark floating belly up, clearly dead.

His balance was questionable when he tried to rise, so he took his time and went to the chair his tormentor had sat in the previous night. Tossing the worthless control box onto the deck, he collapsed into the lounge chair.

* * *

Marvin slowed the boat once the Sawyer Keys came into sight and looked at Mel for direction. She took the binoculars from her eyes and went to the helm.

"That's the Sawyer Keys over there." She pointed to the land on the starboard side, then put the glasses back to her eyes and started scanning the area, stopping at a point on the horizon. Without taking the binoculars down, she pointed in the direction she was looking. "Take it slow. Over there."

Marvin steered the boat toward the spot she indicated and drove forward until she held her hand up for him to stop and set the binoculars down.

He looked at her for more direction, but she remained motionless as if stalking prey. Not sure what to do, she put the glasses back to her eyes and watched the boat.

A dive flag hung limp from one of the outriggers and she could only see one person aboard. Cayenne must be in the water, she thought as she watched the boat. What she needed was proof that Cayenne was poaching lobsters from the site of her coral lease, and inside the boundary of the wildlife management area. She thought about calling the marine patrol again and pulled out her phone. With one eye on the screen and the other on the boat, she opened the web browser and found the number for Fish and Game, but then decided against it. If they arrested her, she had no doubt her father's lawyers would cut a deal and grant her immunity or some other deal for her cooperation. As far as the authorities knew, their only case was against Mac. An arrest would only make matters worse.

"We're going to wait until she comes up and then run close and shoot some pictures," she said to Marvin as she started to play with the settings on her camera app.

Several minutes later, she was startled by the sound of a helicopter coming from the direction of Big Pine Key. The driver of the other boat must have heard it too because she saw him look around and then go forward and pull in the anchor. She watched him through the binoculars as he tossed the anchor on deck and ran back to the helm, where he started the boat and quickly moved away. The binoculars moved from the water to the sky and she focussed on the yellow helicopter cruising overhead.

"Move out to the channel and head toward open water," Mel yelled at Marvin. It looked like the helicopter that was based at Marathon airport for sightseeing tours, not the authorities, but not willing to take a chance she wanted them away from the scene.

* * *

Cayenne heard the engine start while still under the water. With no idea what was going on above, she grabbed her bag full of lobster and ascended the forty feet to the surface. It took her a few seconds for her eyes to adjust to the bright sunlight as she stared in the direction where she thought the boat should be.

Immediately she started to panic, then heard the helicopter and spun in the water, looking for the boat. The charter boat was gone, though, and all she could see were two boat's wakes moving away from her.

She felt exposed bobbing in the waves and there was a chance the helicopter pilot would spot her and without a boat nearby think that she needed help. The paranoia she had felt on the surface left her as she submerged. Although not an experienced diver, the surroundings gave her security. The visibility was excellent and she knew land was only a few hundred yards away. With 1500 psi, she could easily swim toward the cove and Jay's house. The swim would give her time to come up with a story of how she got there. Several scenarios were forming in her head as she started finning in the direction of the cove.

She had almost reached the edge of the mangroves when she heard another boat motor move near her.

* * *

Mac woke, not sure how long he had been out. But at least he wasn't shivering anymore. He looked around, confirming that he was still alone—a foregone conclusion as the man would have checked on him immediately after returning. His throat was dry and his stomach growled—a sure sign that he was recovering from the night in the pen.

He thought about going to the house for water and food, but with the center console docked only feet away, he decided, having no idea when the man would return, that it would be better to get out of there while he could. As he scrounged around the boat looking for any tools that could help him hot wire the starter, he nervously watched the entrance of the cove. He was unarmed and in no condition for another confrontation.

Finally he found what he was looking for: A small box in the console held a screwdriver, wire cutters, and several wrenches. With the largest wrench he slammed the screwdriver tip in the slot where the key would go, and twisted. The ignition fell out, a bundle of wires trailing behind it.

He quickly found two wires for the dead man's switch, stripped them, and twisted them together. Next he located the wires that ran to the starter. The two wires cut and stripped, he moved to the transom, pressed the fuel ball until he could feel the gas inside it, and went back to the helm. The hot wire clamped in the jaws of the pliers, he moved the neutral wire to it and touched them together.

The engine coughed and died.

Again he joined the wires, and this time the engine caught. He released the wires and went to free the dock lines. The boat was free now, and he pulled back the throttle and eased backwards into the main channel before shifting to forward and heading out of the canal.

He scanned the horizon for the boat he expected to return any time, but was distracted by something large against the mangroves. Thinking it was a manatee and not a threat, he looked out to the rental boat he had abandoned last night. He thought about towing it, but didn't want to waste any time. Seconds later, he found the sweet spot for the single engine and the boat got up on plane and started to skip over the small waves as he steered a course back to Wood's.

* * *

Mel yelled at Marvin to slow as they pulled past the Spanish Harbor marker and into deeper water. She had been watching the helicopter circle the Sawyer Keys, but with no boats on the surface, their search was in vain and it moved away. Cayenne had probably been underwater when her boat left, and she thought about going back to search for her, but with the helicopter still in the area, that didn't seem like a good idea.

She knew she had to go back to her dad's and see what was really going on with Mac, and hoped the information she had discovered would make her apology easier. She was feeling guilty at the way she had treated him last night, running off without giving him an opportunity to even try and explain the obvious— how it was all Trufante's fault.

"We're going back to my dad's, OK?" She felt badly about how she had used Marvin as well. But he just nodded and changed course for the small key in the distance.

He must have caught her veiled apology. "You know, sweetie, this is the most fun I've had in ages."

She smiled and punched him gently on the shoulder as he navigated the channel. They reached Wood's ten minutes later and tied up to the same piling they had the night before. Hard to believe it had been less than twelve hours, she thought as she climbed off the swim platform into the knee-deep water and waded to the beach. This time Marvin followed, and she waited at the shore line for him. Together they followed the trail to the house, not sure what to expect as they entered the clearing and looked around.

It appeared deserted. She called out for Mac, but there was no answer. After calling again, she climbed the stairs to the house and went in. There was no one there. She searched the bedroom and went back onto the deck.

* * *

They had been there for several hours and were mosquito bitten and restless, but both knew the consequences of being caught. The two men huddled together in the mangroves, waiting for the sun to reach the horizon. The man started to move toward the roots where he had stashed the scooter the night before.

"It's time." He spat in the mask and washed it with the scummy water. "Hope you know how to use this. He handed him the extra mask and snorkel. It's about half an hour to get out of the bay and to the pickup point. Just hold on and keep your head in the water."

He placed the mask on his face and the snorkel in his mouth. With a nod, he submerged the scooter and waded after it. The other man hesitated but then followed him into the water and held onto his shoulders as instructed.

The scooter pulled the men through the bay at a mere four miles per hour. The pickup point was two miles away, and they had half an hour to the rendezvous. He had timed it perfectly, he thought, as he lifted his face out of the water to check his course. It was hard to see anything, the setting sun placing a harsh glare on the water, but as hard as it made it to navigate, it would also help make them invisible.

There was a compass strapped to the handle of the scooter, but the path out of the bay was complicated, and he needed to follow the landmarks instead of a set course. They were halfway to the open water now as he raised his head, squinted into the sun and adjusted their course to the breakwater. This would be the hardest part of the trip—pushing through the surge as they entered the open ocean.

He pulled the trigger to the maximum speed, hoping the scooter had enough power to propel both men through the waves pushing through the inlet. His head underwater and breathing through the snorkel, he kept the scooter at full speed as it slowly pulled them through the break. Several minutes later he lifted his head out of the water again and looked back at the land receding in the distance.

He checked his watch and realized they still had ten minutes until the rendezvous. With nothing to keep them buoyant, he slowly circled the spot, looking and listening for the sound of the boat coming for them. Again he checked his watch.

This time he realized the boat was late.

From experience he knew that these things never went off on time, but with every passing minute he became more anxious. At ten minutes past the set time, he began to worry even more as he noticed the man on his back start to struggle. There was nothing he could do except circle, so he ignored the man and continued listening for the boat.

A long five minutes later he heard a motor and reached for the cyalume light stick attached to the lanyard of the scooter. He removed the stick, careful to loop its cord around his wrist. If he dropped the light, there would be no pick up, as they would be invisible in the dark. The green light grew brighter as he snapped the stick and held it over his head. The sound of the boat came closer and he breathed in relief that the driver had seen the signal.

Several minutes later he was on the transom helping

Armando out of the water. Once the man was on the top step of the ladder, he climbed onto the boat and had to catch himself as the driver gave a quick glance back to make sure they were aboard before gunning the engines and heading towards Key West. The lights of Cuba faded behind him as he glanced over at the player, who was watching the horizon, getting his last glimpse of his home.

Chapter 20

Cayenne was getting scared as she waited in the mangroves for the sound of the boat to recede. With her head under water she had been fine, the water clear and the current easy, but now that she had to raise it to see what was happening and she found herself surrounded by mangrove roots and branches. Bugs dropped from the trees and then a screach from the brush sent a chill down her spine. She decided to take her chances on who was in the boat and where it was going and swim for the cove.

The clear water soon became murky as she closed on the dock, and something brushed past her, causing her to scream in her regulator. She panicked, using her arms as well as her legs to flail through the water. Her air ran out or at least she thought it had as she started hyperventilating and spat out the regulator. Tears streamed from her eyes as she saw the dock and the feeding frenzy around a caracass. Sharks. Sharks in the water, and she was swimming right for them.

She screamed and turned, swimming frantically for the other end of the dock.

She reached the wooden structure and tried to haul herself out of the water, but the tank and gear weighed too much, causing her to fall backwards twice. She was breathing hard and still crying, but somehow she realized she needed to lose the extra weight, and started to fumble with the buckle of the BC. Finally she gained enough composure to unbuckle it and took off the gear, sending the vest, tank, and weights to the bottom. Without the extra weight, she propelled herself with her fins and jumped onto the dock.

It took several minutes for her to catch her breath and calm down enough to take in her surroundings. The first thing she noticed was that the boats were gone. Then she couldn't help but look at the activity around the cage. She took off her fins and mask, laid them on the dock, and walked over to the cage, where she saw the shark carcass, torn apart at the stomach. Several predators were feeding on the entrails and meat, fighting amongst themselves for the prime cuts. She heaved the contents of her stomach into the water.

Turning away, she looked toward the house. If both boats were gone, it was probably empty, and she could clean up and think up an excuse for being here. She felt confident—as long as she played it right—that Jay would be happy to see her. She could tell him she felt badly about the whole lobster thing and wanted to make it up to him. The captain who had brought her the other day had dropped her off and here she was, ready to make up.

* * *

Mac saw the boat from a distance as he approached, its profile sitting high above the water, and wondered what was going on. Did they circle back after his capture or did he just make a bad call going after them? Mel wasn't like that, though—once she made up her mind, that was usually that.

In any event, he was glad that she was here, and eased the boat next to the larger craft, tying off to its starboard side. There were no fenders onboard the center console, so he pulled the lines tight enough that their rub-rails were touching, jumped off, and headed for the beach.

He was running blindly down the path, both his body and

brain reeling, when he felt the tip of the spear pushed into his stomach.

"Put that thing away," he said as he saw her.

"Good to see you too." She looked him over. "What happened? I heard a boat pull up and grabbed the only thing around."

"Can we go back to the house?" He looked down at his cut-up legs.

"Sorry. Of course." She lifted the butt of the speargun to her stomach and pulled off the tension band.

They walked side by side back to the house, not avoiding each other, but not touching, either. When they reached the clearing, Mac saw Marvin on the balcony. "Can we talk privately?"

"He's in this almost as deep as we are. I think he should hear whatever it is you have to say straight from you. He also uncovered some interesting things about our redheaded friend and her non-profit."

Mac gave her a questioning look.

"Our Miss Cannady was the redhead that suckered Tru to take your boat and poach those lobsters. Where is he, anyway?"

"Tru? I have no idea. I've kinda had a hard night." He went up the stairs, nodded at Marvin, and went straight for the bedroom, where he closed the door. Alone for a minute, he took stock of himself. Small cuts and scrapes covered his legs and feet, and the blisters on his hands from pulling the crab traps were scraped raw, but nothing looked infected. Otherwise he was tired, but unhurt. He headed out the back door of the room onto the small deck, turned on the shower, and soaked under the hot water fed from the solar tank on the roof.

The water soon turned tepid, then cool as the tank ran out. He dried off and went into the bedroom, the towel slung around his waist, to retrieve his clothes. These he hung over the rail to dry in the sun. He faced the door, ran his hands through his thinning hair, and pushed the door open.

The first thing he noticed was Marvin staring at him, but before he could say anything Mel gave the man a stern look. They went outside on the deck and sat facing each other, though Mac arranged his chair using Mel as a shield to screen him.

"OK, so let's go back to the beginning. Tell me about the girls and Tru," Mel said.

"Jeez, girl. I think we're on the same side here ... or at least we should be. Lose the lawyer tone."

"Sorry, can't help myself sometimes. But really. What happened?"

Mac gave her the rundown of his reconnaissance effort the night before. How they had found the girls and brought them back. "That's it for that

Chapter. We came back here, you saw the girls and flipped out. I followed you, ran out of gas, and was taken by that freak on the island."

"So we have no idea where Tru and the girls are?" she asked.

"None." Mac could feel his body now; the adrenaline of the escape was wearing off fast, leaving him more tired than he would admit. "And I'm not really caring about that one."

She dropped the question. Trufante was of no consequence at this point. He would likely bugger up any plan he was involved in. "So that guy on the island is mixed up in this, too?" She asked.

"I'm thinking so, but we have no direct proof of that. He's crooked for sure—smuggling, girls, and all—but I don't have anything to tie him to the poaching."

He thought of the picture he had taken from the house on the island, and went back inside to retrieve it. Back outside, he handed the frame to Mel before sitting down.

She held the picture out. "I'm not sure how much we want to connect them now. This is CIA headquarters and the older man is the current director."

The picture started to become clear. The whole smuggling

thing smelled and now that Mel had identified the man in the picture he knew it must be a CIA operation. There wasn't enough money in smuggling stuff in and out of Cuba to make it worth the risk and expense for anyone without another agenda. The girls were a question, but not really a concern.

"So he's CIA? That doesn't mean he's not mixed up in poaching, though."

"True, but let's get past him for a minute. Cayenne is the logical person to clear you, since she was the one involved. Marvin, why don't you tell him what you found."

Mac turned to face him, wondering what the flamboyant guy could add to the conversation.

"Well, it seems like our redheaded temptress is in some trouble with her little non-profit coral thingy. The books are sketchy and she's using IRS forms, declaring that there is money missing from the business."

Mac wasn't sure what this had to with his problem.

"She's desperate, Mac," Mel added.

Marvin continued, "She's broke, but has to keep the coral farm open for appearances. You know, running a groovy little non-profit to farm coral. Please, she gets invited everywhere because of that - you know it's not her charming personality. Anyway, she's running cash into it from unnamed sources, with no records or receipts, and always keeping the deposits to less than ten thousand. Then she's taking whatever is left out on the back end, declaring that it's missing. It's common for non-profits to do this. For some reason, the IRS gives them a kind of immunity against being responsible with their business. As long as you declare it on the right line of the right form, they let you off without any questions. It's really a pretty sweet money laundering scheme—way above her badly died head."

Mac was impressed by this man's level of knowledge, but still couldn't put it all together. "So how does this get my boat back and clear me?"

Mel took over. "She's probably teamed up with this CIA guy. They started planting the casitas on her coral farm. It's in protected waters but she had a permit to grow the coral here, so a boat sitting on the spot wouldn't be suspicious to the authorities. You know that all the commercial guys steer clear of the protected areas. They must be cleaning up, without any competition. We followed her from Key West this morning and tried to catch her in the act." She paused. "One of those sight-seeing helicopters showed up and started circling. It scared away her captain."

"So she was still in the water when the boat left?" Mac thought back to what he'd assumed was a manatee along the mangroves when he pulled out of the cove. "I think I know where she is."

* * *

"Why we going in there?" Trufante asked as the boat slowed and entered the cove.

"Got some business with the man."

"Ain't no reason," Trufante protested. He knew Commando was going to return the girls. He looked behind him at the three women huddled together on the seat by the transom. They had been having quite the party after Mac left until Commando broke it up and took them. He had come to make another offer for Mac's traps, and saw the opportunity to return the girls.

"You don't bite the hand that feeds you," Commando said as he made the first turn.

"That hand'll bite you back for sure, but that's no reason to tempt it." He could hear at least one of the girls crying now; they'd realized they were going back, he guessed.

Commando ignored him, pulled around the last bend, and entered the cove. He turned toward the girls, now openly crying. "Y'all behave now." His gold tooth gleamed when he laughed.

Trufante slouched in his seat. This was the last place he

needed to be. It had been a promising day and it looked to be a helluva night, but now his plans to party with the girls were ruined. Commando had come by Wood's early this morning, and they had been out all day hanging out with the girls and cleaning Mac's traps out. The fish box was full and he had enough beers in him to keep the smile bright on his face, but now it faded.

A man came out onto the patio and waved Commando over to an empty section of dock. He waited there while they tied off the lines. "Brought you something I think is yours."

"I thank you for that. Who's your partner with the teeth?" he asked.

"Just helped me get some tails is all. He's cool. Got a box full if you're interested," Commando answered.

Trufante sighed in relief that Commando had covered for him. If he just played it cool, maybe he could walk out of here with a pocket full of money. There were other girls he could party with.

The man leaned over and started to pull the girls from the boat. One fought back, but he slapped her hard across the mouth and the others fell in line.

"Go on up and get a cooler to put the meat in," he said to Trufante.

Trufante got out of the boat with his head down and headed for where the man had pointed on the patio. The sooner they got out of there, the better. He found the cooler and took it back to the boat, then hopped into the cockpit and started loading it with lobster. It was overflowing when he pulled the last one out and jumped back on deck.

The man had taken the women and gone in with Commando, leaving him standing there thinking about taking the boat and running. Suddenly a voice interrupted his thoughts.

"Well, look who we have here," Cayenne said as she walked to the edge of the patio.

Trufante put his best smile on. His only option was to do what he did best. "Well hey there!" He smiled at her. He would have rather bull rushed her and pushed her into the water for all the trouble she had caused, but he kept his cool, knowing that if she was here under the blessing of the man, he needed her as an ally. "What brings you here?"

"Same thing as you—no good." She winked at him.

His smile was more genuine now. Apparently she needed him to keep quiet as well. "Quiet as a gator on the hunt," he said.

Chapter 21

"Commando must have taken Tru and the girls. No one else would have known to come here," Mac said as he pulled the lobster tail from the grill and bit into it.

Thinking back, he couldn't believe it had been only a few days since he had come out here. He was hungrier than he thought and finished the tail in three bites. Mel had cooked a half-dozen of the lobsters he and Tru had pulled the other day, along with some food that Marvin had brought up from his boat to round out the meal.

"What are you doing mixed up with that low-life?" Mel asked.

Mac took another tail off the grill. "Guy's got a radar for when someone's in trouble, that's for sure. He came out here with Tru and made an offer on my traps."

"You didn't cut a deal with him, did you?"

"No. I sent him packing. But now he's someone I have to watch. Him and those wanna be gangsters will be after me now." He wanted to change subjects. With less than a week to his first hearing, he needed to act fast.

"The only way I'm getting out of this is to go get that woman and bring her in. Maybe there's some leverage with the guy that has the house out there. If I promise to leave him out of this and forget I ever saw him or his operation he might cut a deal and let me take her," he said.

"It's not going to be that easy. He see's you and he'll want revenge for your escape. And even if he gives you a pass, she's crafty. Even if her business here is a bust, you know her father's not going to let anything happen to her. I'm thinking that Marvin and I head over to Marathon and go talk to Jules. She knows all the players, and you know she'll do whatever she can to help us."

Mac sat back and thought about what she had said. It really wasn't a bad idea. Get her and Marvin somewhere safe, maybe they could even do some good. Then he could go after the girl for insurance. He also knew dealing with the man on the island was going to be more difficult than he'd made it sound.

"Sounds good to me. What about taking me out to the rental boat first." He looked at Marvin. "Your boat use gas or diesel?"

Marvin stared back blankly. "I have people for that," he responded.

"I'll go have a look, and if it's regular gas, you could run me out there on your way and siphon some off. I go anywhere near that island with the center console, he'll know it's me. He only saw the rental boat at night, might not recognize it if I take that one."

"If it's all the same to you, I want you stuck here until we talk to Jules." Mel handed him her phone. "You know how to use this?" When he didn't answer, she took it back and pulled up Marvin's contact info.

"You can reach me here," she said, and handed the phone back to him. "Better leave it off until we leave in the morning or the batteries going to run down."

Mac smiled at her, glad that they would be staying the night.

* * *

Trufante put the cooler on the dock and jumped up next to it.

"You know we could put that back in the boat, go sell it, and party," she said.

Trufante looked down at her and shook his head. "You've got no idea who you're messing with, do you? Guy that owns this boat—" He held up the stub of his finger. "—One of his guys did this. I got no stomach for messin' with that boy. Hell, girl, it's only a cooler of lobster—you in that much trouble?"

She didn't answer, but headed toward the house holding her head low. He followed a few steps behind her, slowed by the bulk of the cooler, and gave the cage with the dead fish floating in it a wide berth as he set the cooler outside the patio door.

Commando and the man were at the bar drinking an amber liquid over ice from crystal glasses. A little of that would surely settle his nerves, he thought as he walked toward them.

"How 'bout a little of that for the help?" Trufante asked as he put his bare foot on the stainless steel bar rail. Leaning on the granite counter, he was about to reach for the bottle when the man slapped his hand away.

"You look a little familiar, my friend. Maybe you can tell me where I know you from before we share a drink," he said.

"Shoot. Could be anywhere. I been kicking around here for a while. Not sure I know you, though." He waited for the promised drink.

The man shrugged. "Name's Jay." He poured from the decanter into an empty glass and slid it down the slick bar top.

Trufante grabbed the glass and set it to his lips, letting the liquid burn against them for a second, as if testing its proof before taking a sip. It was smoother than he expected and he drank nearly all two inches in a single swallow.

"Easy there, partner," Jay said as he topped the glass off. "Maybe you ought to give me a little background, seeing as you're at my house."

Trufante was thinking about where to begin when Cayenne came toward them. "I could use a little of that, too. Not nice leaving the girl out, and you know I always cover my debts." She winked at Jay.

He poured her a glass and, with the drink in one hand and her back against the bar, she turned to face the living room. "Who's your quiet friend over there?"

Trufante followed her gaze to the man sitting deep in the corner of the couch, looking at a magazine. He was dark skinned, his shaven head showing a few days' stubble. Otherwise he looked like an athlete, but with an edge that he couldn't put his finger on. There was a lean, hungry look about him. Apparently Cayenne had noticed the look as well.

"He looks like he could use some company if you're not interested." She started over to the couch.

Jay reached out and grabbed her by the hair. "Don't touch the merchandise. My friend there is none of your concern."

"He's a grown man. Maybe he should speak for himself." She broke free of his grasp.

Trufante knew the look on the man, but couldn't figure out what it was? There was a clue sitting in front of him and he struggled to put it all together. "*Como esta mi amigo,*" he called to the man, and knew he was right when he saw the instant recognition on the man's face.

He turned to Jay and took a stab. "Smuggling ballplayers out of Cuba. Now there's an angle I should have thought up."

Jay looked at the man on the couch, his stare forcing the grin from the man's face. He turned back to the magazine.

"So what of it?" he said to Trufante.

"Just acknowledging a genius is all," Trufante said as he finished his drink. He had no idea where this was going, and he might as well fortify himself if it was going to end badly.

"You look like an intelligent man. Maybe you have a future with me." He turned to Commando. "That is, of course, if you don't need him."

Trufante looked over at Commando and winked, catching him before he spoke. "Of course, *mi amigo*. What is mine is yours," Commando said, and refilled the three glasses, holding his up for a toast. "To new partners."

Trufante ignored the look and toasted. Options were a good thing, and he had just opened a rather large door. He was reveling in his small victory when he heard a scream from the back of the house. Cayenne stormed into view and ran up to Jay.

"What's with your harem back there?"

Trufante looked toward the hall and saw a woman's head poke back around the corner.

Jay got up and put his hands on Cayenne's shoulders. "Just business. You know we have something, right?"

She stood her ground, but before she could respond there was another scream. Trufante looked over to the couch and saw that the man was gone. He stayed at the bar and watched as Jay went to the back of the house, cautious to stay out of sight of the girls.

A minute later he came out with the Cuban in front of him, a gun to the back of his head.

* * *

Mac lay in bed, fighting off the fatigue, determined to wait out Mel. She was almost into a deep enough sleep that he could get up without waking her. Finally her breathing settled and her body jerked. Just a few more minutes now. He counted his breaths until he reached forty-eight, then slid out of bed. She moved slightly and he froze, but then she rolled over and faced the other way.

He pulled on his damp cargo shorts and headed to the door. After a quick look back at Mel, he snuck into the living room and glanced at Marvin, his body lit by the moonlight coming in through the high windows that Wood had put in for ventilation. He was asleep on the couch. Mac had forced him to stay in the house rather than on the boat, where he had wanted to turn on the generator to run the air-conditioning. The sound would carry for miles out here, and Mac wanted to make sure that nothing attracted the man from the island. It was bad enough the three boats were in plain sight, but there was nothing to be done about that.

He slithered out of the house, careful to slide his bare feet rather than step in case the floor squeaked, and stepped out into the night. The wind was still blowing, but that didn't matter for now. Wasting no time, he went down the stairs two at a time and walked toward the shed. He grabbed an old igloo water jug that held a few gallons of water and looked around for a section of hose and a two pronged key used to open gas caps. The moonlight illuminated the path as he made his way toward the beach, swatting mosquitos with his free hand as he went.

He paused at the sight of the moon, hanging two feet over the water, on its way into the dark night sky, casting white light onto the rippled, dark water. But he had a mission and tore his eyes away from the scene as he waded to the boat. He tossed the cooler over the side and climbed onto the deck, using the swim ladder instead of going over the steep gunwale. Hoping that gas cap design hadn't changed, he took the rusted gas key from his pocket and breathed a sigh of relief as it fit the two holes recessed into the cap.

He unscrewed the cap and stuck the end of the hose into the tank. With the cooler open at his feet, he let out his breath and sucked on the end of the hose, waiting for the sting of gas to reach his mouth. Once it came, he took the end of the hose, placed it in the bottom of the cooler, and watched as gas poured from the hose. The cooler was near full and he replaced the gas cap and screwed the plastic lid on.

Hauling the twenty-plus-pound cooler through the water was harder than he'd thought it would be, and sweat stung his eyes as he made it back to shore. He stashed the gas in the clearing behind the kayak and made his way back to the house.

Marvin hadn't moved and he went into the bedroom, where he peeled off his cargo shorts and climbed in bed. At least he had insurance now.

Chapter 22

"What the hell is going on here?" someone yelled from the patio.

Trufante pulled his gaze away from the girls, noticed that the gun remained pointed at the Cuban's head, and started looking for the source of the new voice. A gun fired and he quickly ducked behind the bar and looked back to Jay, who hadn't flinched at the shot, and still held the man at gunpoint. There had to be another shooter.

"Put that gun down—now," the man said, his voice sounding closer. "That's valuable property you're messing with. *My* property."

Trufante peered around the edge of the bar and saw the newcomer walk up to Jay and take the gun from his hand.

"Nice party you got going on here. You couldn't wait until you made the transfer?" He wound up as if to strike Jay, but recoiled at the last second. "Now I'm glad I came in unannounced to pick up Armando here."

He ordered Jay and Cayenne to the couch with one gun trained on them while he used the other to motion for the Cuban to come toward him. "Get those women out of here. I want them gone now."

Jay looked towards Commando and nodded his head. "Take them."

A few minutes later, a loud roar could be heard from the water as a motor started, and the man went to the open patio doors. Trufante looked over the bar and saw the stern of Commando's boat as it dug into the water, the propellors trying to generate enough inertia to push the boat forward.

"Who the hell was that?" the man asked.

Jay got up and ran toward the doors. "It's just a dude I use for supplies. Those girls won't be a problem. Trust me on that one."

The man turned toward him. "You have jeopardized this whole operation. I've overlooked your petty smuggling for years, but now I have the best earner we've ever had standing right here and you've got a party going on." He looked around the room. "There's guns and hookers. I wouldn't be surprised to find a pile of cocaine somewhere."

Trufante wondered if he had missed something.

"It's not like that," Jay said defensively. "Just bad timing. That guy, Commando, is a piece of shit. Just let it go. The player is here." He looked at the man. "And you have the payment?"

The man wound up, smashed the gun into Jay's temple, and stood over him as he went to the floor.

"You get your payment as always—when he gets his first paycheck. You think I'm fronting your ass money?"

Cayenne had moved to the bar and poured herself a large drink while the men fought. Trufante couldn't help but be distracted by her bare leg, just inches away from his face, but tried to ignore the mention of cocaine and the lure of the flesh. He had been in enough bad situations to know he wanted out of this one, so he slid back and crouched at the opening between the bar and the house wall. He couldn't see the men from here, and more than likely they couldn't see him either. It appeared the confrontation was over, and they were working out what to do next.

They moved to the bar and he heard the unmistakable sound of good booze pouring into expensive glasses. "And who might this lovely creature be?" the man asked Jay.

"Hi," she slurred. "I'm Cayenne, but my friends call me Cay. Do you want to be my friend?"

"Well, darling, I'm Norm."

Trufante heard the clink of glasses as they toasted.

"You two want to knock it off before I puke?" Jay asked, and they laughed. "No, seriously, I'd keep my distance from this one if I were you. Been there and done that. Nothing but trouble."

"Asshole," Cayenne spat.

He heard a crash and a scream, and then feet shuffled and someone fell to the floor. With a quick glance, he saw Jay and Cayenne wrestling on the floor. The man named Norm got up from his stool and went to break them up.

Thinking this might be his best chance, Tru sprinted from the bar, making the ten feet to the patio doors. Risking a quick look, he saw Cayenne kicking and pulling at both men as they lifted her from the floor. All three had their backs to him as he ran from the house onto the dock.

He saw the smaller rental boat that Norm had come in on. Risking another glance back, he ran across the dock, jumped into the boat, and went straight for the helm. The engine started on the first try, still warm from its run here, and he went to untie the lines when a bullet grazed his arm.

Ignoring the pain, he rushed back to the helm, staying low as two more shots were fired. Not caring about damage to the dock or boat, he backed hard to port and immediately slammed the throttles forward.

Crouched behind the helm, he was thrown to the deck as the boat careened off the dock. He rose enough to see over the dashboard, aware of the bullets zipping over his head. More shots were fired and the windshield shattered as he ducked and pushed the throttle all the way forward, driving blindly into the cove.

He heard screams from the dock and the start of an engine as the boat scraped against the mangrove-lined bank, then took a chance and looked up to see the last switchback directly ahead. There was more screaming on the dock, but then the sound of the other boat's engine changed and he knew they were in pursuit.

The boat bounced as he crossed his own wake on the last turn before hitting open water, and then he was in the clear. He glanced back, but the other boat hadn't emerged. Wasting no time, he maxed out the throttle and sped away into the night.

The boat was on plane now and he crossed the Cudjoe Channel and sped toward Crane Key. The engine screamed as he pressed the button that raised the angle of the outboard from the water. The top of the propeller was catching air now and he lowered the engine a few inches until it bit.

He hoped this would give him the clearance he needed to lose them in the shallows.

As he passed Raccoon Key, he could hear a boat in the distance and looked up, cursing the full moon. The rental boat, even without running lights, stood out like a cherry on a sundae, and he knew he was not going to lose the faster vessel over open water. He turned to port and aimed toward the Content Keys.

As he closed on the island he looked for the opening into the channel between the islands. It appeared and he cut the wheel to starboard to avoid the partially submerged coral head blocking the entrance. Turning hard back to port, he entered the Content Passage and followed the snaking cut until he hit open water on the other side of the Key.

He looked back as he turned north and realized that no one was behind him. The other boat had either not wanted to risk the shallow entrance to the passage or had grounded.

A large smile crossed his face as he set course for Wood's.

* * *

"Why are you slowing?" Norm yelled over the roar of the three outboards. "He's getting away."

Jay looked at him as he slowed to an idle. "This baby's too big to follow him through there. And getting away with what? He's a lobster-poaching loser. What's he going to do to us?"

Norm wondered how his associate could be so short sighted. "If you thought about the long term for a tenth of a second instead of worrying about your nickel-and-dime smuggling business, you would realize what's at stake here."

The boat idled past the small channel running through the Content Keys, where the other boat had disappeared.

"You act like bringing in the players is a sideline, but when one finally pans out, and I think he's sitting in your living room, we're rich. That guy saw and heard too much," Norm said.

"Well we can't follow him in there. Pretty crafty of him to get by that coral head at that speed." Jay pushed the engines into gear and accelerated past the islands. "But he's going to have to come out the other side. We'll pick him up there."

As he neared the end of the island he slowed again, nosing forward until he had an unobstructed view. "There," he pointed. "That's him."

Norm gripped the leaning post as Jay spun the wheel and pushed down the throttles. The other boat was about a half-mile ahead, but in the moonlight, its outline was clearly visible. They could follow at a distance and see where he went.

* * *

Mac jumped with a start when he heard the boat engine. He must have nodded off, and it took a minute to clear the cobwebs from his head. The engine was louder now, and sounded like it was coming toward them. This was not the kind of neighborhood that had boat traffic during the day; nights were desolate here. He sat up, realizing just how tired he was, and almost lay back down, hoping it was just a chance boater.

Then the motor suddenly stopped. It was too close to be a coincidence, and he could feel his heartbeat in his ears as he lay still, waiting to see if the engine would restart. Mel stirred next to him.

"What are you doing up?" she asked.

"There's a boat out there," he answered as he put his feet on the ground and slid the wet shorts back on. "It just stopped. Sounds like they're by the beach. Stay here, I'll go have a look."

"Like hell." She got up, dressed quickly, and followed him out the door.

Mac looked at Marvin on the couch, still snoring peacefully, and went past, Mel close on his heels. They left the house and went downstairs, where he grabbed the machete stuck in a pole by the door and scolded himself for leaving the shotgun on the boat.

"Wait."

He watched as Mel went toward the shack, opened the door, and emerged with a speargun.

"How about you point that at the ground," he said, as she ran into his back. "And slow down. We have no idea what's out there." He started down the moonlit path. Before they broke from the brush into the clearing, he stopped suddenly and crouched down with her at his shoulder.

"See anything?" she whispered in his ear.

"Not yet. That boat's in the way." He pointed at Marvin's cruiser. "You stay here. I'm going to crawl over there and get a better view." He slid on his belly underneath some scrub palm trees and into the clearing with the boat trailer and kayak. Once clear of the brush, he got on his hands and knees and crept toward the water using the mangroves for cover.

He heard the unmistakable sound of a man sloshing toward shore and prepared to attack. Mel had probably heard it also, and if he knew her, the speargun was cocked and ready. He was just about to charge the intruder and yell at her to shoot when he saw Trufante emerge from the water.

"Shit. What the hell are you doing here?" He stood and walked toward the Cajun. Mel came out of her hiding place as well, speargun at her side.

"Got to talk." He looked back over his shoulder.

Mac picked up on the movement. "Did anyone follow you?"

"They were, but I was crafty and lost them in the Content Passage."

Mac was not convinced. They might not have followed him through the tricky channel, but that didn't mean they hadn't skirted the island and followed from a distance. "Come on. Let's at least get off the beach." He looked back at the boats tied to the pile. There were too many to go unnoticed.

He led them through the path to the clearing and started up the stairs to the house. "Should be able to see anyone coming from the back deck."

He led the way through the house and out the back door of the bedroom, where the palm trees opened up and allowed a 120 degree view of the water. After tying a bandana around Trufante's arm to stop the bleeding from where the bullet had grazed him, he looked straight at him.

"All right. Spill it."

"Shoot. You talking to me like I done something wrong," Trufante whined.

"When was the last time the three of us were together and you *hadn't* done something wrong?" Mel accused.

Trufante looked down. "I might have got us into this, but I got some intel now. Might be able to save this mess." He told them about the scene at Jay's house on Sawyer, about the new man, the player, Commando ... everything he could remember. Mac noticed Mel perk up at the mention of the player, and his mind started to calculate how to get Cayenne. Knowing she was there made this more interesting. He had to get her out of there before the men realized she was a risk and eliminated her.

He put a finger to his mouth to quiet them. Over the rustle of palm fronds blowing in the breeze, the sound of a motor could be heard in the distance. He waited to see if it was coming towards them.

Chapter 23

Mac knew they were in trouble as soon as he heard the engines stop. On the small island, with no weapons besides a speargun, a shotgun, and a machete, they were bound to be outgunned, and could be easily cornered. The wood-framed house, though built to withstand a hurricane, was no match for bullets. With nowhere to go and no way to defend themselves, his first concern was to create a distraction and get Mel and Marvin to safety. Marvin's boat, although not as fast as the triple outboard he'd heard, was fast enough, and with a small head start would make the mainland safely.

He turned to Mel. "You've got to grab the boy and go. We'll figure some way to keep them busy so you can get out of here. I'm not sure what it will be but as soon as you see it, go for Marathon and tell Jules what's going on." He was not sure what the sheriff would be able to do about the CIA agents, but she was the only card they held.

"What about you? We can all get away," she said.

"Tru and I are going back to the house on Sawyer Key to get that woman. That's the only way I can clear my name and get the boat and house back. Without her, I'm going to jail."

Mel didn't say a word—a sure sign that he was right. She gave him a quick hug and went to wake Marvin.

"What're we gonna do?" Trufante asked after she left.

"Hell if I know. Somehow we need to draw them away from the boats and give those two enough time to get out of here." He led them to the front porch. "They have no idea what we've got going on here, so they'll be cautious and a little jumpy." He paused, the idea for a distraction still not coming to him.

Then he turned to Mel. "Work your way around the outside of the cove and wait. Whatever we come up with will be big enough to get their attention and lure them away from the water. Find a spot where you can see if they leave the beach. As soon as they move, go for it." He handed her the shotgun, but she wouldn't take it.

"I'm better with this and it'll probably do more damage than that pea shooter." She patted the speargun and pushed Marvin in front of her.

Mac watched them as they cautiously kept to the perimeter of the clearing before slowly moving toward the trail. Mel would be all right, he knew; her companion, he wasn't so sure about.

Once they were out of sight, he turned to Trufante, an idea starting to form.

"You know when you shorted the solar panels?"

"Goddamn. That spark about made my hair stand on end."

"They didn't come here to dance, and they know we're here. Both boats are sitting out there. We've just got to get their curiosity going and they won't be able to resist coming after us." He went downstairs and walked across to the shed. The lights were out—part of the 12-volt system that he had disabled—but enough moonlight shown into the small room to see. The wires were fried from Trufante's encounter with them, but the batteries would still hold a charge. Wired in series now, they would produce 110 volts—enough for a big spark, and that was what he intended.

He went inside for some tools and took them to the battery bank against the wall. The ten batteries were sitting adjacent to each other on two shelves, and he remembered from rewiring them which was the last in the series. He traced the wire to the charge controller and opened the box. There wasn't enough light to see the colors of the wires.

"Find me a light or some matches," he called to Trufante.

While he waited, he went to a pile of fishing gear and pulled out a five-foot-long aluminum-handled gaff. Trufante was back with a box of kitchen matches and he lit one, its yellow flame producing enough light to see the wires.

The match was almost to his fingers when he reached the charge controller. He dropped the stub on the floor and lit another. It caught, and he could see the color of the wires clearly now. The red wire removed, he attached a longer length of wire to it, and brought the cable outside, where he stripped six inches of insulation from the end. He pulled the rubber grip off the gaff and wound the wire around the handle.

With the handle back in place and covering the bare wire, he could hold the gaff without fear of shocking himself. If this worked, the entire gaff would be energized as soon as it contacted anything that grounded it, causing a huge spark to shoot from the end.

The matches gave him another idea. It was risky, but if it worked it would give them enough time to escape.

He pulled out an old fishing reel from the shed and started to peel off the lead core line. He then went to a pile of traps nearby and pulled a section of black nylon line, brittle from years in the saltwater. He threaded the fishing line through the center of the trap line, weaving it in and out of the braided line, and then tied it to the gaff. With an old oar he suspended the gaff over the solar panel array.

Hoping the coating on the fishing line would burn like a fuse, he lit the end of the line and watched as the red glow ate its way toward the trap line. It was working, and he estimated he had about two minutes until it burned through the trap line and the gaff dropped on the panels.

"Ready?" he asked Trufante, who held the shotgun. "Don't

shoot unless you have to. I don't want them to know where we are. Go for the boat. I think they'll still be looking around the beach, but as soon as this blows I bet they'll move. They should come running to see what it is, and we can grab the boat and make a run for it then."

Mac counted in his head as they moved carefully down the trail, hoping he hadn't misjudged the men. His count was in the eighties when they heard an explosion and the sky lit up. Small pops and flashes continued as the energized gaff shorted itself against the panels.

A minute later he heard an engine start, and pulled Trufante off the path. Mel must have seen the men leave the beach and gone for Marvin's boat. Relieved they had escaped, he moved backwards into the scrub palms, his arms shredding from the abrasive branches. He squatted on his heels and held himself in a crouch. Trufante was breathing hard next to him.

Footsteps and muffled voices came toward them. Mac got low and put his head down as the men passed by. He knew they were pros from their cautious movements, but as long as they were moving toward the clearing, his plan was working. A long ten seconds later, he moved out of the scrub and ran the hundred feet toward the beach. Trufante was on his heels as they entered the water and waded to the boat.

"Go. I'll be right behind you." He turned and ran back to the clearing, grabbed the cooler of gas he had siphoned from Marvin's boat, and ran back into the water.

They climbed over opposite gunwales and seconds later had the motors started. They were underway. He had chosen the triple outboard, knowing the guys chasing them wouldn't be able to outrun him with the smaller boat.

"Pull all the lines," he yelled to Trufante, hoping the other boats would drift off in the current.

Mac looked out to the open water in the direction of Marathon and saw only a small dot on the horizon. In another minute, Mel would be out of sight. He turned the wheel in the other direction and headed toward the Sawyer Keys, hoping to get in and out with Cayenne before the two men figured out what was happening. *They'll go back to the island, that's where the woman and the ballplayer are,* he thought as he pulled into the main channel.

They would have to be fast to get the girl out while the CIA men were still here. He had nowhere near the weapons he expected they had and Trufante was undependable in a fight. He looked back at the island as he turned west and could still see sparks, but they were accompanied by smoke now. With a whoosh, the sky lightened and he realized the shed must have caught fire. With a grimace, he realized that it would soon reach the house.

There was nothing he could do about it now, but if the buildings were on fire, it probably meant that the men were running from the blaze. Which, in turn, meant that they were on Mac and Tru's trail. He leaned forward on the throttle and the boat planed out, skipping over the waves.

Another loud whoosh came from behind him, but he refused to look back, knowing the house was gone.

* * *

Mel steered straight for the hump in the Seven Mile Bridge—the safest path through the ink black water. There were faster routes, but none were safe at night, the shallows and obstacles invisible in the dark. They entered Moser Channel and went toward the center span, where she cut the wheel to port and ran parallel with the bridge toward Boot Key.

Minutes later they passed Pigeon Key and she counted six openings before turning right. They cruised below the spans of the old and new bridge and turned left, heading toward the blinking marker, which they passed a few minutes later to enter the channel. She reduced speed and followed the markers to the first dock on the left.

The boat banged twice against the rub rail as she came in too hot, and it was a long minute before Marvin could reach the dock lines and secure the boat. She cut the engines and grabbed Marvin's phone, cursing herself for not giving this one to Mac. Without her contacts, her ability to get things done was limited. Frustrated she went into the maps app and entered 'sheriff.'

An icon came up and she clicked through to the phone number. Wishing she had taken the time to call earlier, but knowing it was dangerous to stop the boat so she could hear, she waited impatiently while the phone rang. A deputy answered and took her information. She could only hope he was relaying it to Jules. A few long minutes later the phone rang.

"Jules. It's Mel," she started. "We need your help." She waited while the sheriff woke up. "Can you come to Pancho's Fuel Dock?"

She started pacing the minute she hung up the phone. There were a lot of moving pieces, and she needed to determine what to divulge and what not to.

* * *

With a nervous glance over his shoulder, he slowed as they approached the rental boat still anchored where he had left it. The boats touched and he grabbed the side of the anchored boat.

"Hold her!" he yelled at Trufante, unscrewing the top from the cooler and dumping the gas onto the boat. He tossed the empty jug in when he was done. It took several tries to light the match in the wind, but one finally caught and he tossed it into the boat as well.

The blast hit them as he slammed the throttles to their stops and looked behind him at the boat now engulfed in flames. Without looking back, they sped toward the inlet hoping the fire would slow their pursuers. The boat skidded sideways into the mangroves as he misjudged the switchback guarding the entrance to the cove and took the turn too fast. He eased the throttles, but only enough to get back on course, and steered toward the dock. Trufante jumped out and tied the boat off while Mac ran to the house.

"Take the boat around to the back side!" Mac called over his shoulder to Trufante. "They could show up any minute."

He barged through the doors and found the living room empty. Not sure he had made the right decision, he made his way into the house and started searching for the red-headed woman, his fatigue fueled by adrenaline. If he could get the woman out of here and back to Marathon before the men returned he might have a chance to clear himself.

He moved to the back of the house, shotgun leading the way, and heard grunting coming from behind a closed door. Pretty sure of what he would find, he kicked the door in and entered the room. The two figures in bed grabbed for the sheets to cover themselves as he loomed over them.

"Get dressed now!" he yelled at Cayenne, who tossed the covers aside and reached for her clothes. The Cuban remained in bed. "You too," he called to the player, deciding on the spot that it would be better to take him as well. He could be more valuable than the woman if it came down to a parlay with the CIA men.

The man looked at him, not sure what he was after, and Mac searched his memory for any Spanish.

"*Vamanos,*" Trufante called from behind him, and the man instantly grabbed his pants and dressed. A few minutes later they were down the hall and on the way out the doors.

That's when they heard a boat.

From the sound of the engine, Mac guessed they were in the switchback and would appear in a few seconds. Trufante had started around the house, the player following. Cayenne screamed when Mac grabbed her arm and yanked her around the corner and out of sight just as the boat entered the cove. He could see the boat as it entered the cove, and he pushed the group further around the house, hoping the shadows would conceal them. He looked at Cayenne and the Cuban, gauging whether either looked like they would cause trouble. The man looked confused, but the girl was another matter. Mac knew from the trouble she had caused already that she was volatile, and out only for herself.

He stepped behind her, moving as if he were trying to slide deeper into the shadows, and placed his arm around her neck, applying pressure to her carotid artery. She was out almost instantly, and he supported her body and slid her against the side of the house. Another look at the Cuban, who nodded at him as if to say that he knew not to cause trouble, and he turned back to the dock.

The men on the dock were shouting at each other as they tied up the boat and made their way to the house. It would be only a few minutes until they discovered that the man and woman were gone. Mac looked toward the brush and the path they had cut the other night. There was about ten feet of clear space between them and the building, but with Cayenne still out cold, he decided it was too risky to try to cross the open area.

Even if they weren't seen as they crossed, the sound of the group moving through the brush would attract their pursuers.

Chapter 24

Concealed by a bush, Mac stayed low and peered around the corner of the building. Both men left the house each carrying a rifle in each hand. They moved down the dock and loaded the weapons into the boat.

"Go back, get the boat, and bring it around the island," he whispered to Trufante. "Stay clear of the inlet so they can't see you if they leave."

He watched the man as he sprung cat-like across the clearing and entered the brush. Mac held his breath until the branches settled back in place.

"Where are you going?" the older man suddenly yelled toward Jay, who was heading to the house.

"We need something bigger, just in case. I'm getting the rocket launcher."

Mac turned back toward the men and tensed. The older man was walking from the dock to the patio, right toward where they were hidden. He readied the shotgun and braced to attack if he rounded the corner, but instead, the man stopped a few feet away and pulled out his phone.

Mac stayed ready, but relaxed when the man started to talk. The call sounded like it was all business, telling the man on the other end that his delivery was going to be delayed. *Must be the player*, Mac thought as he looked at the man huddled next to him, his eyes wide. Despite his muscular stature, he could tell the guy was scared. He hadn't spent more than a few minutes around him, but he sensed his fear of the two CIA men.

The call ended and he yelled, "Jay!" he called to the other man, who had just set a large weapon in the boat.

"What?" he turned. "We've got to go. They can't be more than a few minutes ahead of us!" he yelled back.

"Do you know where they went? There's a lot of water out there and with the range of those boats, they could be anywhere. Let's be logical. You have that punk's number?"

"Commando? What's he going to do? Damned junior gang-banger skipped out on us already," the younger man said as he walked toward the older man.

"We need eyes on the mainland. I saw the big boat heading toward Marathon when that explosion went off on the island. These guys are craftier than you're giving them credit for. A rookie wouldn't set up a diversion like that and then come here. They would have run. There's more going on here than you're telling me. What's with the girls, the party? Pretty unprofessional, if you ask me." He paused. "You have that police scanner? Might be a good idea to see if they get the authorities involved."

"Yeah. I'll get it." Jay pulled his phone out of his pocket and handed it to the other man who took it, pressed the touch screen, and put the phone to his ear.

Someone answered and there was a heated conversation, but it was in Spanish, and Mac had little idea of what was being said. He looked at the player who was listening, but realized they would need Trufante to get any kind of translation. The only thing he knew was they had called Commando, and that was bad for Mel. He needed to warn her, but the phone she had given him was on the boat.

Now the men were ready to leave, and he heard the engine start. There was nothing he could do except watch them go and hope Trufante would pull in right after they left.

The boat was around the first bend and out of sight when he left the cover of the house. The player remained with Cayenne, too scared to move, but that was fine. There was nowhere for either of them to go. He started searching along the side of the dock while he waited for Trufante. If he was going to get out of this mess, he needed them to know he had both the girl and the player as bargaining chips. If they reached Mel first, there was no telling if they would kill her or take her hostage to exchange for the player.

His leverage would be gone if they got to her first.

He looked up from the dock box he was tearing through and saw the bow of the boat appear around the bend. Lines, hoses, and a few gallons of oil were scattered on the deck, but he couldn't figure how to use any of them to create a spectacle big enough to bring the men back to investigate. The oil was not going to ignite, but he saw two tiki torches mounted on the rail at the entrance to the dock. They would make a fire, but not big enough to attract the men.

He needed a bigger fuel source.

Trufante had the boat idling by the dock when he looked up from the materials and saw the three engines on the transom.

With only seconds left before the men would be too far away, he dragged the hose to the tiki torches, left one end draped over one torch, and grabbed the other from its holder. After dumping the fuel onto the deck and rails, he lit the first torch with a lighter sitting next to it.

"Tie it off and get those two onboard," he yelled at Trufante as he passed, dragging the other end of the hose behind him. The Cajun gave a questioning look, but he ignored it and kept moving. He jumped onboard, pulled the hose to the transom, took the pliers he had found in the dock box, and started to unscrew the cap-nut from the long stainless steel bar that supplied fuel to the engines.

Trufante came towards them, Cayenne slung over his shoulder and the Cuban following behind. Mac went to help, and Trufante leaned over the boat to hand the limp body to him. She came to just as he took hold of her and started flailing. Her nails clawed his face and he dropped her as one found his eye. She was kicking and screaming as she broke free and ran past Trufante, who reached out to grab her.

"Get her!" Mac yelled to Trufante. Leaving him to it, he went back to work. He pushed the end of the hose over the stainless steel tubing and went to the helm. Then a scream broke the silence and he looked up.

Cayenne had been heading into the house when Trufante grabbed her and started to drag her back. They were past the open end of the hose, leaning on the wick of the torch, when he turned all three keys at once and cringed as the starters ground on the flywheel.

Nothing happened.

He kept the keys turned and listened as the starters began to lose battery power. It took a second to figure out it would take a minute to push the half-gallon of gas needed to fill the hose to its outlet. Just as he was about to give up, gas started to spray from the end of the hose, turning the torch into a flame thrower.

Cayenne broke loose and ran back toward the house, leaving a startled Trufante staring at the flame. He ran back toward the dock and pushed the player onto the boat ahead of him.

Mac released the keys, but the fire was roaring now. The fuel he had dumped ignited and a fireball lit the sky, increasing in size as the suction of the fire, seeking oxygen, pulled the remaining gas from the hose.

"Get rid of the hose and put the cap back on the fuel rail!" he yelled at Trufante, who had just jumped on the boat.

Mac looked at the house, partially engulfed in flames, trying to find Cayenne. The volume of gas in the hose had burnt itself out, but everywhere he looked small fires were raging, the wind adding the oxygen they needed to flourish. He was about to give up on the girl when he saw her run out of the house, smoke streaming from her hair.

Without a thought, he jumped from the boat and took off down the dock after her, but could only stand idle as she ran screaming off the patio into the water, landing in the remains of the cage. Her head came out of the water once, the fire extinguished. Then she screamed again, the sound cut off as she was dragged under.

There was nothing he could do to help her as he watched the water churn. An arm reached out as if for help, but it was the last sign of her.

The house was burning as he pulled his eyes from the carnage and ran to the boat. Trufante had the fuel rail re-assembled and was trying to start the boat when he jumped on and went to the helm.

The starters had lost their urgency as the batteries drained, and he realized the engines had also lost their prime.

"You've got to squeeze the balls," he yelled, and went to the transom, where he pushed Trufante out of the way, opened the access panel, and started working the primer ball for the first engine. He grabbed the other two, one in each hand, and squeezed until he felt them harden.

Back at the helm, he closed his eyes as he turned the key. From the weak sound of the starters, he knew he only had one shot to get them started. The fire was spreading to the dock, consuming the wooden structure, and he thought about abandoning ship just as the first engine caught. The old dock wood was burning fast and he felt the heat on his face as he pulled back the throttle for the single engine and backed into the cove.

With a whoosh, the palapa ignited. No time to start the other engines.

He looked back as they entered the switchback and saw the tips of the flames just reaching above the palm trees, a huge column of smoke streaming from the island. One at a time, he started the other engines and headed around the last switchback where he stopped the boat. He needed to draw them into a trap. If he could make it look like he was fleeing the burning island they would follow.

* * *

"Holy crap," Jay yelled. "That's coming from my island." There were three smoke plumes on the horizon. The one from the island they had left had almost died out and there was a small cloud over the water. But he stared at the other fire, which was putting off a huge black cloud of smoke, and it looked like it came from Sawyer.

Norm turned to look, but didn't change course.

"Shit. We searched the house. They must have been hiding in the brush or something. Somebody had to start it."

He thought for a second. There was something else at play here. "What about Armando? You locked him and the girl in the fun room ... right?"

Norm didn't wait for an answer. "Call that punk and make sure he takes care of whoever's on the other boat. We're going back." He turned the wheel hard, changing the boat's course.

Norm ground his jaw as the boat sped towards the fire. "It has to be the man from the island, looking for revenge. But we can't risk losing Armando."

As they rounded the marker and turned west toward the smoke plume, Jay could see the fire clearly. He turned around, picked up a rifle, and chambered the first round.

Whoever did this was going to pay.

* * *

Mac turned to Trufante as they waited at the inlet, searching the horizon for the boat to return. "He heard a phone call the man made to Commando in Spanish." He looked over at the man on the other side of Trufante, who was looking around like a scared

179

animal. "See if you can get anything out of him."

Trufante turned to him, and the man became animated, talking quickly and using his hands for emphasis. The conversation was way past the phone call.

"Give me something," he told Trufante.

"His name's Armando and he's a baseball player from Cuba," Trufante started.

"How about something that might help," Mac growled.

"The man called Commando and told him to find whoever was coming in on that boat and hold them."

"You sure he said to hold them and not kill them?" Mac asked.

Trufante turned to the player and asked. The man shook his head.

"He also says he's scared of them and wants to go home," Trufante said.

"Well, tell him we'll help. We need him on our side," Mac responded. He turned to the player and nodded, giving him his best reassuring look.

"There!" Trufante pointed.

Mac followed his gaze and saw the spec on the horizon. It was hard to see with the whitecaps and breaking waves, but there was definitely something there, and it looked like it was coming toward them. Slowly it began to grow, and Mac waited until he was sure they would see him pull out of the cove. He timed their approach confident he had a large safety margin. The three 275-hp engines mounted to the transom behind him would make it impossible for the single-engine boat to catch them.

Then he remembered the call to Commando.

"Text Mel and tell her that Commando is working for these guys and might be after her." He pulled Mel's phone out of his pocket and handed it to Trufante. "What was the flamers name? Melvin? Oh. Marvin."

The boat was getting close now, and Mac knew they would

see him. He pushed down the throttles and left the shelter of the inlet. The engines roared as he adjusted the speed to 3,300 rpms— the slowest he thought they could run and stay on plane. Once he was sure the boat was in pursuit, he could slowly increase speed if he needed until he was ready to lose them or lead them into a trap.

They had rounded a bend and started toward the channel on the west side of the island when he dared to look behind. The smaller boat was following, and he adjusted his speed to match theirs. He had to let them think they had a chance of catching him, or they could take a more direct route and reach Mel first.

Chapter 25

Mel was grinding a path into the dock when Jules pulled up fifteen minutes later. Without her phone and contact list she was frustrated and there was nothing she could do until the sheriff arrived. She saw the police cruiser pull up and was at the SUV before Jules could open the door.

"These CIA guys are smuggling baseball players from Cuba and they're the ones that set Mac up. Well, them and Cayenne Cannady. We have to do something now. Mac's out there and could be in trouble!"

Jules got out of the car, took out a notebook, and leaned against the fender. "Let's slow down and start at the beginning. Are you all right?"

Mel ignored the question, already frustrated with the time lost. She was not here to give a statement; they needed to take action. "Can we do this later? I have a boat here that we can take back to Mac's."

She started toward Marvin's boat without waiting for an answer. The phone vibrated in her pocket, but she continued to the boat.

"Mel!" Jules called from behind her. "We can't run off half-cocked. You have to tell me what's going on. I have resources we can use if he is in danger."

Mel was on the boat now, casting off the lines. She turned to

Jules to renew her plea when she saw a man walk behind her and place a gun against her head. Two other men appeared from the side of the building, rifles extended, and moved cautiously toward the boat. Marvin clung to her as the men approached. One man jumped down onto the deck of the boat and pointed the barrel at them while the other stood guard on the dock.

"You too, little lady." The voice sounded familiar to Mel. He lifted his head to reveal his face, hidden below the wide brim of his hat, and her stomach clenched as she realized it was Commando. With the barrel of the gun still at Jules's head, he pushed her forward to the edge of the dock. "Let's go, time for a little payback for all the trouble you've caused me over the years."

He stepped back, cocked his leg, and kicked her in the back.

Mel watched her fall forward and land hard on the dock. She went to help, but the man with the rifle pushed her back toward Marvin.

"Yo. Untie the dock lines and take the SUV back to the bait house. I'll take them and meet you there," Commando said as he kept his gun on Jules and waited for the man on the dock to leave. "Cover them," he said as he jumped onto the boat. "Phones." He held out his hand and waited while they passed them to him one at a time.

He kept the one Mel handed him, but threw Jules's over the side. "Just in case your boyfriend calls. I have some words for him."

One of the men walked toward the SUV, got in, and started the engine. Once he had pulled out, Commando focused on the trio in the boat.

"Lemon swirl here is going to drive." He laughed at his own joke and waited for Marvin to move to the helm. "You two over there." He motioned with the gun barrel to the bench seat by the transom.

Mel sat with Jules against her. She looked toward the deserted dock for help, but it was receding into the distance as the tide took the boat into the channel. Despite the peril, she had been through situations like this with the sheriff before, and knew that if she could stay calm, an opportunity would present itself.

That thought became harder to swallow when Commando wound up and smacked Jules across the side of her head with the butt of the gun. She collapsed into Mel and he came toward them.

Mel winced, thinking she would share the same fate, but he reached for the sheriff's belt and removed it. With the gun still pointed at Mel, he grabbed a handful of zip ties from a compartment on the belt.

With a tie in his mouth, its ends stuck together to form a loop, he grabbed Mel's wrists, slipped the tie around them, and pulled. He reached for another tie and leaned over to secure her feet when she caught Marvin's eye.

She blinked hard several times to get his attention and then moved per pupils in an exaggerated motion, trying to communicate with him using her eyes. He got the message, grabbed the fire extinguisher strapped next to the helm, and started toward Commando, who looked up at her just as Marvin was about to wind up and strike.

There must have been something in her eyes—either a reflection or a tell—because he pivoted, extended the gun, and fired.

Without looking back, he turned to Mel, finished placing the tie around her ankles, and pulled hard. After trussing Jules, he went to the body on the deck. Marvin was moaning in pain, grabbing his thigh. Blood spurted from the wound— a sign that he had hit an artery.

"Don't!" she yelled at Commando, who fired again.

"Can't be too careful," he laughed and went for the helm. Blood coated the deck and it looked bad for the man.

Mel looked around, desperate for help, but there was no one on the water; the high winds had kept the casual boaters and commercial fishermen off the water. Jules started to stir and Mel bent over and whispered in her ear to stay down. Marvin was still on the deck clutching his thigh, but there was nothing she could do for him.

Feeling helpless, she scanned the land and water for anyone or anything that could assist them, but as they passed through the harbor and turned into a commercial-looking canal, the prospects turned to zero. The canal led to Monster Bait, the home base for Commando and his crew. They passed commercial lobster boats, docked on each side of the narrow waterway, all deserted. The deeper they got into the channel, the more industrial it looked and the worse she thought their chances for escape were.

Commando pulled up to a rickety dock loaded with traps and line, where the man with the rifle stood waiting.

"Off," he said as he waited for the men to tie off the boat before he shut off the motor and pocketed the keys. "I think you two remember where the chum shed is."

Mel cringed at the thought of revisiting the shack where Trufante's finger had been ground down. Nothing good awaited them there.

"Yo. Take the boy and hold him with the girls," Commando said to the man as he stepped onto the dock and waited. "You two. Help him."

Mel and Jules grabbed Marvin under his arms and pulled him to his feet. He was unconscious, his body limp. "He needs a doctor."

"Shit. He's going to be the special of the week out on the reef. Maybe I'll call it Lemon Swirl. What's with the hair, anyway?" He laughed and looked straight at her. "Now let's go."

Just as they stepped off the dock and started onto the crushed coral trail leading to the chum shack, his phone rang.

It seemed like a reprieve had finally come as she listened to the one-sided conversation. Whoever the caller was, he was clearly the boss. Commando said another "Yes sir" and then hung up.

"Change of plans, looks like the fishes out there will have to wait for the Lemon Swirl." He looked at the other man. "Lock him up with the girls and get the car."

* * *

Mel landed against Jules as Commando shoved her into the back seat. She could do nothing but watch as he went around, got in next to Jules, and stuck a piece of duct tape over her mouth. Mel's mouth was already taped.

"Travis's house," he ordered the man behind the wheel. "You remember where it is?"

The man nodded and the sheriff's SUV started onto the driveway and picked up speed as it hit the road.

"Hold it down. You don't want to get a ticket," Commando snickered, and jabbed Jules in the ribs.

Mel watched out the window, wondering where Mac was and if he would be able to figure out where *they* were. Maybe he would have sense enough to call the sheriff's station and they would realize Jules was missing. She wasn't sure what that would accomplish, but she knew she had to stay positive.

The car turned onto US1 and headed south toward Mac's street. A highway patrol car passed in the opposite direction and she swore the driver waved. Commando laughed—he must have seen it too. The driver pulled into the center turn lane and waited for traffic before turning left. At the end of the block they pulled into the crushed coral driveway in front of Mac's house.

"Go check out the house and set up the sniper rifle on the canal. We don't want any unexpected guests," Commando said to the man in the passenger seat, who took the long rifle and went toward the back of the house. "You stay here and watch them," he said to the driver. "I'll check things out." He opened the door and got out.

Mel looked at Jules after Commando was out of sight,wondering if she had a plan. Jules was calm, but Mel could tell she was alert. Her eyes told her to relax, that and wait.

Chapter 26

The three men huddled together, their backs against the leaning post, swaying with the motion of the boat in a futile attempt to stay dry. The bow crashed through the waves, sending spray flying, but despite knowing the boat would ride better and drier if he increased speed, Mac knew they had to take the pounding to allow the other men to follow.

He turned backwards to make sure they were still there and had to search the whitecaps to see the spray kicked up by the other bow as it smashed through a wave. Back behind the partial protection of the windscreen, he traced a line with his finger on the plotter, showing Trufante the course he had chosen.

"That's dicey. You know that channel's not marked. There's rocks and shoals all through it," Trufante yelled.

"Have to risk it," Mac said. His biggest fear was that their pursuers would tire of the chase and decide to take a short cut to reach Marathon and get to Mel first, if Commando hadn't found her already. He needed to take the fastest route to the Atlantic side to keep his pursuers from bearing off. If they stayed on the Gulf side, there were several routes the other men could take. But on the ocean side of the bridge there was only one, and he would have the upper hand with the faster boat. He suspected that these were not the kind of guys that would stay back and lick their wounds. They would follow and hopefully take his bait. Once he reached the ocean side, he could increase speed and slowly pull away. He would stay close enough to let them see him enter the Knight's Key Channel and hopefully lead them into a trap.

"Text Mel and tell her to get Jules to set up an ambush or something at the vacant fuel dock down from Burdines." The red brick building had been abandoned for years, and would make a perfect location to trap the men.

Trufante looked down at the phone, went to the last message he had sent and started typing a new one. He finished and hit send, then handed the phone back to Mac. The boat was approaching the area where the lone green marker should be, the Niles Channel Bridge just visible in the distance. He could do nothing except move his eyes from the chart plotter to the screen of the cell phone. Neither gave him the results he was after.

Finally the phone vibrated and he looked down. There was a response from Mel for him to meet at his house. He texted back OK, wondering why she had not used his plan, but knowing he had no option but to trust her.

They were within a mile from the bridge now. He saw the green marker and kept it to port, slowing the boat in order to navigate the difficult and unmarked channel. Howe Key and the shoal adjacent to it came into view, and he moved the boat into the center of the channel, then turned around to see how close the approaching boat was.

The smaller boat had closed the gap, having the benefit of being able to follow and letting the lead boat navigate. Mac looked forward at the unmarked channel, worried that if they couldn't increase speed quickly their pursuers would soon be in gunshot range.

Just as the thought crossed his mind, he heard a bullet pass over his head.

He accelerated and steered toward the deeper water adjacent to Summerland Key. They were close to the bridge now, and he was able to line up the bow with the center span and increase speed. It was safer to go under the bridge at a higher speed with the current conditions. Too slow and the waves and current—always stronger near the structures—could toss the boat into one of the piers. With the throttle down, he cleared the bridge and headed toward deeper water, clearing the Newfound Harbor Keys, then turned to port on a course parallel with the land.

The shadow of the land mass blocked the wind and the water calmed. The waves were two feet lower now, and he was able to push the throttles down and accelerate toward the lights of Marathon in the distance. When they reached the Bahia Honda Bridge he knew he would be standing on his dock in less than twenty minutes.

"Text Mel back and give our ETA at twenty minutes. Tell her to let Jules know about the boat following us. I'm going to lose them as soon as we hit the channel. The police can take it from there."

His thoughts moved to Mel as they entered the Knight's Key Channel and he slowed for the no-wake zone, passing the gas docks and the empty building. It was the perfect spot for an ambush and he wondered again why they had decided against using it. It was too perfect and he thought about the brevity of Mel's message. He was about to make the turn into the canal leading to his house when he saw a glint of light from the window of the spare bedroom upstairs.

He slowed and moved the boat toward the seawall, out of sight of the window. There was no reason anyone would be up there. The room was used only for storage, but it had an unobstructed view of the entrance to the canal. Just then the light shut off.

"Why we stopping?" Trufante asked.

"Something's wrong up there. Go on and scout it out. I saw a light from the bedroom upstairs." Mac nosed the boat to the seawall.

"So? Mel texted you to meet her here, why the games?" Mac

glared at him and Trufante shrugged his shoulders and jumped up onto the concrete seawall. "How do I find you?"

"I'll be here. If Mel is there and everything is OK, get your butt back here fast." Mac watched as he disappeared in the shadows.

* * *

Mel flinched when the man turned to look at her and Jules in the back seat. They sat in front of Mac's house, bound and gagged. She looked over at Jules, who was sitting patiently. Mel knew Jules's training was telling her to wait for an opportunity rather than waste energy, but she was impatient and fought her restraints, the nylon ties twisting and digging deeper into her wrists with each movement.

Jules turned to catch her eye and from her facial expressions, Mel thought she was trying to tell her something. But she had no idea what. She did at least follow her lead and stopped struggling with her restraints. The man looked back again, as if sensing something was going on, then turned around and picked up his cell phone.

He was focused on the screen, the bill from his hat covering his face limiting his peripheral vision. Jules nodded to her, but she had no idea what she wanted. She nodded again as if to say *NOW*, and Mel did the only thing she could think of. In one swift movement she aimed for the soft part of the guy's skull below the crown, leaned forward, and head-butted him from behind. He didn't react, almost as if he hadn't noticed. Jules wasted no time and swung her legs around and over the seat, forcing as much space as the restraints binding her ankles would allow and spread her knees over his head.

Mel saw her muscles tense as her body lifted off the seat and twisted against his neck. He seemed to wake from his daze for a second, but then there was a loud snap and he fell limp.

Mel sat back, giving Jules enough room to pull her legs off the man and swing them back. They sat in silence for a minute, waiting for retribution, either not trusting that the man was dead, or fearing that Commando had heard the fracas and was heading back.

Finally they realized no one was coming and looked at each other. Still unable to communicate, Mel used her nose to release the door locks and they fumbled with the handles, each falling from the car and landing on the gravel driveway. She looked around for cover and saw the neighbor's landscape adjacent to their house—a feature Mac had never bothered with. She inched toward the cover of the bushes. Jules followed behind her, and both women were soon concealed behind a row of oleanders. They were panting through the tape over their mouths; their noses straining to keep up with their bodies' need for air. Slowly their breathing came under control and they looked at each other, wondering what to do next.

Then they heard the unmistakable sound of a shotgun chambering a round and the motion sensor security light came on.

"Ladies," Commando said as he moved toward them.

Mel rolled to her right, trying to regain the cover of the bushes, but a foot stepped heavily on her back. Commando stood over her, pointing the shotgun at Jules. Her body relaxed, about to accept her fate, when something entered her vision from the neighbor's driveway, moving fast and launching itself into the man.

The weight on her back was gone now and she crawled to her knees, trying to see what was happening. A tall man was wrestling their assailant on the ground. She saw Jules move toward them and followed her lead. The tall man was in trouble, underneath Commando now, who wound up to hit him.

Mel saw Jules tense and slam her body against him. Her momentum was enough to knock him off the other man. Now he lay within striking distance, and Mel thought that if it worked once, why not again. She leaned back and with all the force she had left, head-butted him. He fell lifeless onto the driveway. She looked from him to the man on the ground, who smiled at her.

"Hell of a head you got there," Trufante said.

She grunted through the tape over her mouth. He smiled, showing his grill, and peeled the tape off, then went to Jules and did the same.

"Never thought old Alan Trufante would be saving the sheriff," he said.

"Don't get all cocky. We're not done. Now cut these ties."

Trufante went to Jules and reached in his pocket for a small knife, which he opened to cut the ties.

"Drag his body out of sight," Jules called to Trufante as she picked up the shotgun and released the rounds to see how many remained.

Trufante hauled the body into the bushes while Jules reloaded. They regrouped in the neighbor's driveway, out of sight of the house and away from the motion sensor.

"There's one more armed man in there. He's got a sniper's rifle with a scope," Jules started to brief them.

"I've got to get back over there." Trufante pointed to the seawall on the opposite side of the canal. "Mac's waiting with the ballplayer."

"That must be what the sniper is doing. They must have lured him here to take him out and get the player back," Jules said. "Go on back there and tell him to wait until I flash the dock lights three times. Then it'll be safe and he can come over. Until then, that sniper's got eyes on him."

Trufante took off and was lost in the shadows. "What now?" Mel asked.

"We've got surprise and a weapon now. That guy's sitting up there focused on the canal, waiting for Mac to come in. If he hasn't been down here yet, he has no idea what happened."

Mel thought for a minute. "You want me to distract him and

you can sneak up and take him out?"

Jules laughed. "Listen to you, Melanie Woodson. Your dad would be proud." She looked at the house. "I can't legally ask you to risk yourself like that, me being the sheriff and all."

"No worries. Just tell me what to do."

The plan was simple. Mel gave Jules a few minutes' head start, then walked up to the front door like she lived there. She ignored the auction notice and tried the handle. The door was locked, but she reached down and lifted a shell on the stoop, took the key and opened the door, careful to make enough noise to be heard and distract the shooter from Jules, who should be in the master bedroom by now. She banged around downstairs until she heard footsteps above her.

"Mac." She yelled, as if she expected him to be here. Nothing happened. The footsteps seemed to stop. Jules had told her that under no conditions was she to go upstairs, but nothing was happening.

She started to climb the steps, again calling Mac's name. No sound came from above, and she slowed her ascent, worried the gunman might be waiting for her. She was almost paralyzed with fear as she reached the door at the top of the step, and fell backwards when the gun went off.

She caught herself on the rail and realized the shot was not at her.

"Clear," she heard Jules yell, and climbed back up and opened the door. It didn't move at first, but she pushed harder and saw the blood pooled on the floor.

Chapter 27

"Tie it off," Mac yelled at Trufante as he stopped the boat at the seawall and jumped onto the dock. He didn't look back as he raced to the house, took the back stairs two at a time, and pulled the door open. Not sure what to expect, he crept through the bedroom with the shotgun ready, then moved to the door and nudged it enough to see through the main room to where Mel and Jules were.

They stood by the door, hovering over a man lying in a pool of blood on the floor. Mel turned and rose as soon as he entered, and he ran to her. Holding her tightly, he let her warm tears drip down his neck as they embraced. Finally she pulled away, and he saw the distress on her face.

"We've got to do some damage control, and fast," Jules said. "There's three bodies here and several shots were fired. Commando was an amateur, but these CIA guys are pros and there's always a good chance that a neighbor will call about the gunshots." She went to the land line on the counter, lifted the receiver, and started to dial. "I'm going to call this in and say that I'm in pursuit and following them to the bait house. That'll give me some backup to help Marvin and the girls and it ought to give you enough time to clean this mess up and get out of here. If you're here when the police arrive, they're sure to think you did it. And if I'm here and you're not in handcuffs, my credibility is shot.

It's better if we're all gone."

"Where are they?" Mac asked, ready to take action. He looked around the kitchen and living room, his eyes stopping on the body at the top of the stairs. "What about the others?"

"One's in my SUV downstairs. The other is in the bushes. We moved him out of sight," Jules said.

"Tru's out back. We'll toss both bodies in the canal." Mac started out of the room with Mel and Jules behind him.

"Wait," Jules called, the receiver still in her hand. "You can't be here, Mac. You've got to run. You're lucky it's my day off and the station doesn't know where I am. I've gone as far off the reservation as I can without risking my job. I'm sorry."

Mac knew she was right. With a court date looming and the water muddied further by the dead bodies at his house, he had no chance with the law. Time was the only thing that was going to clean this mess up.

"No worries. You've done more than I could have expected." He went to her and gave a quick hug, then turned and left the room with Mel following behind him. Once down the stairs, he headed toward the boat, wondering how much fuel it had.

Mel followed. "I want to talk to the Cuban. He's a victim here. We can't abandon him," she said and climbed onto the boat.

Jules called from the driveway before he could ask what she intended.

"Help me out here."

He left Mel and Armando on the boat and went down the side of the house, with Trufante close behind. They went to the car and pulled the body out. He glanced at Mel and Armando, in an animated conversation on the dock, and hoped that Mel could help the guy figure out what to do. Then they hauled the dead man to the seawall, dumped him, and returned to the bushes, where Jules stood over the body.

"It's that punk Commando," Mac said.

"Yeah, I know. No loss there. I'll see if I can buy you some time." She went for her SUV, started the engine and pulled out of the driveway.

They hauled Commando along the same route as the other man. Before they were able to reach the water, a phone rang. They stopped and dropped the man, looking around for the source of the sound. It rang again and Mac looked at the dead body, then reached into a pocket and grabbed the phone. Mel and Armando must have heard it as well, and ran up to them.

With nothing to lose, Mac hit accept and then pressed the speaker button. They gathered around him. A voice called out in Spanish and they looked at each other, heads shaking and looks blank. Mel was about to speak, but Mac put a finger to her mouth as Armando stepped forward.

"*Bueno*," he said.

The voice on the other end unleashed a tirade.

Mel grabbed the phone, disconnected the call and went to the settings screen. "Location services are on. If they're CIA, they can track where we are." She turned toward the water and threw the phone in. "We don't have much time."

"Get the boat ready. I'm going to grab some gear." Mac went for the downstairs door. "Tru, check the gas. We've got to figure out where to go."

Before anyone could answer, they heard a boat in the canal. Mac cursed and ran to the dock. The rental boat sat in the mouth of the canal, its bow wave just lifting it as it settled to an idle and started to approach.

"It's them!" he yelled.

"What now?" Mel asked, fear evident in her voice.,

"I've got an idea." Mac looked back and forth between the boat across the canal and Commando's tattooed legs in the driveway. Any way this went, he was either dead or in jail.

His thought was interrupted by the sound of a whistle getting louder as if coming towards them and he looked up as something passed over their heads. Shock came over him as he followed the projectile and stood motionless as it smashed into the upstairs window.

The back half of the house erupted in flames as the missile exploded. Anger burned through him, but he forced himself to calm down enough to evaluate the situation. With the well-armed men sitting in the canal, just waiting for a chance to take them out, and the police sure to pull into the driveway at any minute, they were cornered. The plan to take the boat would be suicide with the CIA men sitting in the canal.

He looked around for a way out and saw the sailboat at his neighbor's dock. "We've been needing to make a change for a while. Maybe this is our opportunity," he said to Mel, who was staring at the house.

Mel followed his gaze to the boat. "As long as we help Armando, I'm game. Guess he's not too impressed with what he's seen of America. I tried to explain that he could request political asylum, but he wants no part of it." she said.

Mac wasted no time now that they had a plan—if you could call stealing a sailboat and returning a refugee to Cuba a plan. He looked at the dock and the three outboards on the boat.

"You ready to redeem yourself?" he asked Trufante.

"What up?"

"Take the boat and blaze out of here. Keep going until you hit the Bahamas or whatever. Just draw them off us and give us some time to get out of here."

"What am I supposed to do then?"

"You've got the numbers for my traps. Keep the boat. Why not? That'll keep you in beers 'till we get this sorted out." Mac didn't wait for an answer. He gave Trufante a quick nod and ran to the back door, avoiding the falling pieces from the burning deck.

"Grab the passports and whatever we can hock," he yelled back to Mel, who was following him. He looked back at Trufante who was on his belly, working toward the dock and handed the shotgun to Armando, hoping he would know what to do.

He went to the house without waiting for an answer, entered the workshop downstairs, and started piling gear on the floor. A timber crashed by his head and he moved faster. If he could make one more dive and recover his cache, he could wire his neighbor money to pay for the boat and they could live large in the Caribbean until they figured things out. Maybe they'd be back soon … maybe not.

A motor started and two more followed in quick succession, and he knew Trufante was about to pull out. A shot fired and he heard the shotgun chamber another round and fire again. Armando must be covering Trufante's escape. Then a burst from a machine gun fired and he heard an engine accelerate. They must have taken the bait and followed.

With a tank in one hand, a bag with his dive gear in the other and a pole spear wedged under his arm, he went back outside, giving a quick glance backwards. The fire was through the roof now and he knew it was the last time he would see his house. Mel was already at the dock next door, Armando by her side. Sirens were audible in the background now. Mac heaved the tank over the chasm separating the boat from the dock and dropped it onto the deck. He followed and waited for Armando to hand him the gear. At the helm he pushed the start button and, without waiting for the engine to warm, set it into reverse and pulled backwards from the seawall. He could hear the roar of the triple outboards in the distance and smiled. Trufante would do as he had asked.

"Ready?" He looked at Mel.

"Yeah," she answered with a determined look.

Mac pushed the throttle to forward and turned the wheel hard to port. The boat followed his commands slowly, the engine not nearly as powerful as the outboard though it turned. As soon as the boat was positioned correctly, he headed toward the harbor. He couldn't help but smile as he pushed the throttle forward and motored toward open water.

Chapter 28

Norm turned the wheel over to Jay and climbed the stainless steel structure supporting the T-top. The faster boat was nowhere in sight, and his only hope of finding them was to get a better vantage point. His shins crashed against the piping as he reached for the fiberglass roof, blindly looking for a handhold to haul himself up with. The boat hit another wave, the action accentuated by his height, and he reached for anything to keep him from falling.

His hand hit the base of an antenna and he hauled himself onto the roof. The top was unfinished and the rough surface scraped his skin as he crawled onto his belly, and then his knees. He dared not go to his feet without something to support him, but even on his knees his vantage point allowed him to see the water beyond the light. There was only a sailboat out past the tower. The boat they were chasing was no where in sight. Another wave battered the small boat and he grabbed for the antenna mount and missed. Instead of the base, his hand grabbed the fiberglass whip, which splintered in his hands. The next wave put him back on his belly and he climbed down to the cockpit and stood next to Jay.

"I lost them. Pretty sure I saw a sailboat out past the light," he said, pointing where he thought he had seen the mast tip. "Can't see anything, and with these conditions we can't outrun them. Maybe keep pace, but we won't catch them. As soon as it's dark, any course change and they would easily escape."

He looked at Jay, his jaw clenched and eyes fixed on the light, and knew he had lost them. Time to cut his losses and start cleaning up this mess. His long-time accomplice was now the weakest link in the chain. Norm had been trained to put his emotions on hold when action needed to be taken, and went to the place in his mind where he could operate without thinking.

He raised the gun but decided against using it. If a wave hit, his aim would be compromised and he could damage the craft. He needed another weapon, and looked around the boat for anything he could use.

Suddenly he saw the eight-foot antenna he had tossed from the T-top lying near the bow. Holding the stainless steel railing he went forward, ducking as each wave crashed over the bow and soaked him, to retrieve it. Looking back at the helm, he saw Jay's gaze still focused on the waves in front of them. They were so big you had to drive through almost every one, planning the best angle to assault them. It would keep the other man busy for as long as he needed.

He picked up the antenna and made his way back to the shelter of the cockpit, where he took a position behind Jay. The thin fiberglass snapped easily in his hand as he broke it roughly in half, discarding the thinner end. With the base in hand, he stood back and braced himself, timing the waves to assist him, then lunged forward, slamming the ragged end into Jay's back.

He crumbled to the deck, blood pooling around him. Norm pulled the spear from his body and hauled his inert form to the transom, where he pushed him overboard. Discarding both halves of the antenna, he caught the wheel as the boat spun and changed course toward the towers marking the entrance to Sister Creek. He could use one of the remote channels off Boot Key to clean up the boat and figure out his next move.

It was a bad result for the Nationals, but for him personally, he knew he would survive. There might be another opportunity though, as The White House had just announced the resumption of diplomatic relations with Cuba and he suspected it wouldn't be long before the trade embargo was lifted. He had a plan to turn the Guantanamo Bay base into a Vegas type strip. This might be the right time to get out of the smuggling business.

* * *

Mac dared a glance behind them as he steered toward the coordinates he had entered in the GPS. He hoped his memory had served him. The two - seven digit numbers were deceiving. The first four were easy. The entire area was around the 24 degree latitude and, depending how far west you went, either 80 or 81 degrees longitude. It was the final three numbers that identified the spot, and he had long ago committed this site to memory. He looked around, but they were alone in a sea full of whitecaps. It looked like Trufante had succeeded, and he silently wished him luck.

He scanned the horizon again and still saw only whitecaps. There was no pursuit, the CIA men having followed the power boat. He turned to Mel.

"Take the wheel," he said, and pointed to the waypoint on the screen. She knew what to do from there, and he went to the cabin and pulled out the dive gear.

He bounced around the cockpit as he tried to strap the BC and tank to his back. The seas were coming in fast and hard, throwing him off balance every time he tried to lift the weight of the tank off the floor.

"Where do you want to drop anchor?" Mel yelled over the roar of the wind and noise of the waves smashing the boat.

Mac had her stay close to the waypoint, using the chart-plotter to stay close to the spot. "We can't anchor in this. You're just going to have to keep circling. I'll take a bag down and inflate it when I'm ready to surface. Then you can motor over and pick me up." He finally managed to close the velcro waistband and buckle the strap.

Armando came over and helped him adjust the tank on his back.

He slid across the wet deck to the transom—the only place on the boat he could exit without the coated wire guardrails interfering. His body jammed in the corner to remain stable, he put on his fins and mask and grabbed the spear. With his right arm he swept behind him to find the regulator, which he put in his mouth, and, in one movement, he rose and fell over backwards to enter the water. Immediately his body stung from his blistered hands and the scratches on his legs, but he fought through his injuries and started his descent. It was like a different world the minute he was under water. The turbulence above ceased to exist, the angry seas replaced by tranquil water. He warmed as he descended slowly, the eighty-degree water like a hot tub after the wind-blown spray they'd endured on the way out. Clearing his ears every few seconds, he dropped through the water column, trying to even out his breath from the excitement of the chase and exertion of getting in the water.

He reached the bottom and checked his gauges. Calculating fifty minutes at the seventy-five-foot depth, he went to work. In his previous efforts to find his stash, he had followed a grid using standard search procedures. But this was his last shot, and he had to think outside the box.

He adjusted his BC and floated several feet off the bottom, picturing in his mind how the site had looked before the anchor had torn it apart, and imposed that image over what he now saw. He had assumed before that the anchor had dropped the coral heads where they were, not thinking they could have been dragged across the bottom. This area of the reef had no defined walls or ledges with which to orient yourself. It was a forest of coral heads, sponges, and hard bottom; one area was almost indistinguishable from another. The three corral heads had been his landmark, so he had naturally gone to them.

Now he thought he might have been wrong. The two heads remained where he had last seen them, leaning next to a third. But what if the third structure was not part of the original cluster? He looked around and saw similar lone corals scattered over the bottom. He checked his watch and air, then looked at his compass and followed a westerly course, thinking that the predominant sea conditions were from the southeast, and that a boat with a stuck anchor would have backed down in that direction to free itself. Slowly he started swimming a search grid, staying ten feet off the bottom in sixty-five feet of water to aid his air consumption and add to his bottom time.

He checked every coral head as he circled the area, but their bases were all undisturbed. The incident had happened within the last six months, and he expected some growth, but the craters where the two heads had been should still be visible.

A line became visible above the sand, moving slowly towards a coral head, and he couldn't help but follow the black grouper, finning closer for a better look; as intent on finding his stash as he was, it was hard to ignore a large fish. He had brought the spear more out of habit and to use as a pry bar than to hunt, but he couldn't resist the challenge. And he wasn't sure how the boat was provisioned; they might need the meat.

If he had just been hunting, the fish would have been on his stringer by now, but in the time wasted thinking about it, the grouper sensed him and all he could do was watch it tense, and with two sweeps of its tail fin, speed away.

Just as he was about to look away and resume his search pattern, a lone coral head in the path of the fish caught his eye. It was not where he thought, but the ocean bottom often appeared to shift depending on current and visibility; the bottom could look one way on a Monday and completely different on Tuesday.

Perhaps he'd been seeing it wrong the entire time. Invigorated, he quickly swam into the current toward the coral head. He was using more air than he had wanted, but the excitement of possibly finding his cache overruled his better judgement.

A long few minutes later he arrived at the coral head, out of breath, and checked his gauges. The hard swim had cost him, and the needle kissed the red zone, showing five hundred psi of air left. Not a lot at this depth, and he would need a reserve to ascend and wait for Mel to find him. With no time to lose, he held the inflator hose over his head with his left hand, released air from his BC, and descended to the bottom.

He knew he was on the right spot as soon as his eyes came level with the lone coral head. Beside it, he could see where the other heads had been. The boater must have dragged them to where they now lay.

He was down to two hundred psi now—minutes from running out of air—as he stuck his hand under the coral head. Something was different, and the space felt smaller than before. Frantic to recover anything, he took off the BC and let it rest on the ground. Without the bulk of the vest and tank, he jammed himself as deep as he could into the opening and moved his hand back and forth in the small cavern.

He was about to give up, when his hand brushed against what he thought was a rock. But it moved too easily, and he grabbed it. Without the time to look, he stuck the object in his BC pocket, slid back into the vest, and inflated the BC. Working with both hands, one to secure the vest and the other to add some air to the BC, he started a fast but not dangerous ascent.

Twenty feet from the surface he reached in his pocket and pulled out the inflatable marker, took the regulator from his mouth, and pressed the purge button. The red material retained the air and quickly floated toward the surface. With the regulator back in his mouth, he sucked for another breath that did not come.

His lungs burned as he kicked towards the surface and spat out the regulator as soon as his head broke the surface. A mouthful of sea water greeted him as a wave broke over his head. White-capped waves crashed around him and he realized the seas were at least a foot bigger than when he had entered the water.

He spat out the sea water and gasped for air, sucking as much as he could before another wave slammed into his face. Using his fins, he pushed himself out of the water and took a deep breath, which he held while he fumbled for the inflator hose, recovering it and breathing the air held in his lungs into the bladder. This gave him enough buoyancy to float above the water, and he looked around, using his fins to turn.

Mel was a hundred yards away, the waves too high to see the small red float. He started to swim toward the boat, but a minute later realized that the current was against him. He would never reach it, and with the wind and seas crashing, she would never hear him if he screamed.

The only option was to signal her.

He pulled the buoy toward him and stuck the red fabric on the tip of his spear, which he extended over his head. The float lost its air as soon as it was out of the water, but stuck on the end of the long shaft it was several feet out of the water, he hoped she'd see it. All he could do was rest on his back and let the BC support him while he waited.

* * *

Mel circled the imaginary mark, keeping one eye on the seas and the other on the chart plotter. She had been able to communicate with Armando by putting her hand to her head as if she was searching and repeating 'rojo' as she scanned the water. He got it and looked vigilant as he held the winch by the helm for support.

She didn't have a watch but she used the clock on the chart-plotter screen to estimate Mac's bottom time. He hadn't said how long he was going to be, but she expected that at forty-five minutes he would be out of air soon. She turned back into the waves to continue her circle and saw the red buoy above the water.

Slowly she approached the red float, careful to stay to windward so the boat would be moving away from Mac instead of crashing into him. Leaving the wheel for a second she grabbed the PFD from its bracket on the safety rail and handed it to Armando, hoping he would know what to do.

The seas were way too rough for her to idle up and let him climb the ladder. They would have to stay to keep him in the lee of the boat and haul him in. Again she circled, this time closer. Armando threw the life preserver into the wind, but despite his pitching arm, the float fell short and he pulled it back in.

She breathed deeply, knowing their pursuers had taken the bait and followed the power boat and that Mac was fine floating in the water. There was no reason to panic. Once more she circled, turning as close to him as she dared.

"Throw it!" she yelled to Armando, hoping he understood.

He wound up and tossed the ring sidearm like an inside slider and landed the line across Mac's head, the float landing several feet past him.

She set the boat in neutral and turned her back to the wheel as she watched Mac retrieve the float. Armando started to bring the line in and she breathed in relief as Mac approached. Just as he reached the ladder, a huge wave hit the bow, throwing her to the deck.

When she looked up, Armando was nowhere to be seen. Now both men were in the water, and she had a second of panic before she saw Mac pull himself up the ladder.

Chapter 29

Mac unbuckled his BC and let the tank drop to the deck as he watched Mel throw the PFD to Armando. He removed the rest of his gear and went to help, taking the line from her hand and pulling the man toward the boat.

Armando appeared dead in the water, and Mac didn't know if the man was unconscious or could not swim. The wind was pushing the boat's higher profile faster than the smaller body in the water, and the man's head was being submerged under the water as he was pulled towards the hull.

Things were looking worse and worse.

Suddenly, he saw the figure cough and spit out a mouthful of seawater. Mac hauled the line into the boat, no longer anxious that the man had drowned, but wanting to get him out of the water as quickly as possible.

"Unbuckle the guard rail and grab him as soon as he's close enough!" he yelled to Mel.

She went to the rail, unclipped the two wires surrounding the boat, and leaned toward the water. Mac pulled harder now and the man came to her.

She grabbed him by the shirt collar, but between his weight and the forward movement of the boat, Mac doubted she could hold on much longer. He went to the helm and searched the unfamiliar console in front of the wheel, finally finding and activating the auto-pilot. The system began to fight the water, trying to keep the boat on course in the pitching seas.

He went to her side, reached over, and grabbed the man. "See if you can find a boat hook or gaff!" he yelled over the noise of the engine and waves.

Mel let go, giving him the weight, and he had to pause to appreciate her strength. After only thirty seconds, his blister-covered hands were starting to cramp. He looked forward and realized they had only seconds, the tower marking the reef loomed over them.

Mel bumped against him as a wave pushed her off balance. He grabbed the boat hook from her hand and reached for the man's waist. The waves bounced the end of the hook away from its target several times before he was able to place the small hook into Armando's belt. Twice he released his death grip on his collar to test the hook.

Both times it held, and he released his grip.

"Grab two dock lines!" he called to Mel, keeping an eye on the man in the water as she searched.

"Here. You want me to hook his legs?" she asked as she put the end through the preformed loop, making an adjustable lasso.

"Yeah. One's good." He watched her open the circle and toss it over the side.

The water immediately closed the opening in the line before it reached his leg, so she pulled it back and tried again. This time she tossed it well forward of his leg, landing the loop around him and allowing the force of the water to move it into place. She pulled the end of the line slowly until it hit his foot, then pulled back hard like she was setting the hook in a big fish. The loop grabbed and she looked at Mac.

"Tie it off and use the other to loop his arm," he directed as he looked forward to check their position. The light blinked ominously several hundred yards away. They had only seconds now before the hull would be destroyed by the reef.

Mel tied the line to the cleat, wincing as if she felt the man's pain as the line pulled his leg. Again she formed a lasso and worked it through the water, catching his arm.

"Now switch with me. Careful or we'll tear his limbs off." He moved back and took the line tied to Armando's arm in one hand and waited to transfer the boat hook to her. She slid in front of him. The man screamed in pain as the pause in the transfer allowed the line attached to his foot to jerk. Mac tried to ignore him and focus on the work. He took the line in his hand, turned to the winch, and removed the jib sheet looped around it. With the two loops on the winch and the bitter end in his hand, he moved back to Mel and took the boat hook from her grasp.

"Now untie the line on his feet and yell when you're ready. Then pull as hard as you can." A gust came up, forcing him to scream as the wind whistled through the rigging. He waited for her to release the line and when she nodded, pulled with both hands, trusting her to be able to handle Armando's legs. He pulled on the line around the winch and on the boat hook at the same time, using his knees to brace himself.

The man screamed again, but the line was coming. He looked toward Mel and saw she was doing her part.

With a huge effort and the last of his strength, he pulled and leaned over the side to grab the man's belt with his hand. He was almost in the boat now. One more pull and the three bodies crashed onto the deck.

Mac was breathing hard, but he forced himself to his feet and moved to the wheel, ignoring the pain from the torn blisters on his hands. Despite the rough water and overcast conditions, the water was so shallow he could see coral heads passing to the side of him. A white mooring ball, used by snorkelers, passed to port, and he knew they were in imminent danger.

From the corner of his eye he saw the depth finder reading eight feet, and he grabbed for the spokes of the wheel to disengage the autopilot. The wheel spun free and he had to react quickly to grab it before the boat spun beam to the waves. Once the boat was under control, he turned 180 degrees and pointed the bow toward deeper water. He watched the depth finder as it climbed out of single digits into the high teens. Finally out of danger, at least of grounding, he engaged the auto-pilot again and slumped forward.

A hand touched his shoulder and he jumped and turned to see Mel standing by his side.

"I can keep watch for a while. Why don't you take a break for a minute?"

"What about Armando?" he asked as he looked at the man on the deck.

"He'll be OK. I think he dislocated his arm and he's in some pain, but he'll live." She moved to the wheel.

He needed to decide on a course and looked towards the ominous looking ocean reflecting the last of the sunlight. In the distance, a freighter made its way east, marking the edge of the Gulfstream. Commercial traffic used the current to save fuel, and the best indicator of where the stream was currently running was the closest eastbound boat. Past that point, he knew they would face hours of wind and weather, but on the other side they would be in the Bahamas, and could use the shelter of the island chain to hole up and regroup, then maybe sail south toward the Dominican Republic and points farther south.

He knew the boat could survive the trip and was sure he could as well, but after the man-overboard drill they had just completed, he was worried about Mel and Armando. But he also knew they had no choice. He needed to reach the Bahamas and clear customs before his name was red-flagged for stealing the sailboat and skipping bail. There was also the matter of the fires and dead bodies, and he hoped Jules could help there.

He kissed the back of her neck and gave her shoulder a squeeze before taking the wheel.

Enjoy this Preview of Wood's Harbor

Wood's Harbor

Mac swatted the no-see-ums swarming around his face and rubbed his salt-crusted eyes. The coating felt like sandpaper. Finally he removed enough of the crystals to squeeze one eye open. The glare of the sun made him close it immediately. He tried to move, but his legs resisted the effort. It took him a long minute to realize they were entwined in mangrove branches and covered with debris. It was a struggle to sit up, so he lifted his knees instead, and in the process gained enough wiggle room to slide out of his cocoon. He forced himself to squint through his one good eye and crawled across the muck to the tide line where he splashed water on his face. It was salt water, but it was wet. He continued until he was able to open both eyes.

His vision was clouded from the salt and sun, but he forced himself to survey his situation. Surrounded by mangrove roots, he saw pieces of the wreckage in the brush and tried to remember what had happened. He gazed up at the sun, high in the sky, and realized it had been close to sunset the day before when time had stopped; he had been out for almost eighteen hours. His memory came back in bits and pieces as he moved above the high tide line and sat amidst the tangle of roots and brush to think about the last few days. It came back slowly. He remembered the sailboat fighting each wave as he tried to steer it into the raging Gulf Stream. Then the rest of the memory flooded back, startling him to alertness.

He gained his feet and looked around for Mel and Armando. They had been with him on the boat, but his last memory was the life raft and the terrified looks on their faces. The mast had snapped, taking his attention away from the drifting lifeboat. That was all he could remember. The trio had escaped the corrupt CIA agent and headed to the Bahamas, a trail of dead bodies and destruction behind them, a 'borrowed' sailboat beneath them. It had been his insistence on running that had left him stranded and his stubbornness that had convinced him he could navigate the huge waves and current of the Gulf Stream. He looked around with remorse. It may have cost Mel and Armando their lives.

Mac pushed the thought from his mind and tried to gain his feet. His arms and legs were covered with open cuts and scrapes, the current target of the invisible bugs, but his wounds showed no sign of infection. He was forced to crawl, the dense vegetation not allowing him to rise. With two choices, the open water or the brush, he chose the water. There was likely a search going on and he would have to be careful to remain out of sight. If he was found on US soil, he would surely be arrested.

First on the list would be the poaching charge. He recalled the image of the heiress, Cayenne Cannady, red hair ablaze, as she burned at the smuggler's haven. The temptress had suckered his friend and first mate, Trufante, into using his boat to poach lobsters. The black cloud that followed the Cajun mate was above them that day. The pair had been caught, the boat traced to Mac and confiscated along with his house. He shook his head. Focus on the present. It was better to stay invisible until he could figure things out. He worked through the brush to the shore but couldn't get the two faces in the lifeboat out of his mind. The question of whether he was responsible for Mel's death dominated his thoughts.

The winds had calmed, reducing the seas to a light chop. From the debris scattered in the mangroves, he could tell it had been a good blow. Parts of a boat, fishing nets, plastic bottles and trash were scattered in a wavy line along the tide mark or in the branches, some, two feet off the ground, where the surge from the wind-blown waves had deposited them. He looked around for anything useful and found a pair of mismatched flip-flops and a half-full water bottle which he drained. Able to stand now, he set his shoulders and lower back into a stretch. The sun had moved behind him. He knew he was somewhere back in the Keys facing the Atlantic Ocean. There were hundreds of miles of mangrove-covered shores in the island chain running from Homestead through Key Largo, past Key West to the Dry Tortugas, and he had no idea just where he had been marooned.

He turned towards the sun and started half-walking and half-wading west through the mud, the best choice as he figured the six-knot current of the Gulf Stream would have pushed the wreckage north or east. At least he was still in the Keys. The last place he needed to enter civilization was Miami or points north. He had been walking for an hour, by the position of the sun, but doubted he had covered more than a mile. He fought for each inch. Finally he saw a high-rise appear over the brush and sighed in relief as he recognized the lone condo standing guard over the entrance to Key Colony Beach. He studied the shoreline and moved back into the cover of the brush as a boat appeared from the inlet, then looked inland to find a place to rest until sunset. Coco Plumb Beach, the long stretch of sand leading to the channel, was too busy to approach in the daylight. Even if he wasn't identified, he looked like a hobo and would be reported by the residents.

He crawled under the cover of a small tree. His thoughts turned inward as he fought hunger and thirst. The initial shock had worn off. He could feel every scrape on his body, salt stinging open wounds as it dried. Mel was back in his thoughts. Had she survived? Where was she? Armando was a concern, but he would be handled as a political refugee, given the best care American taxpayers could afford. Mel would be treated as a criminal. He waited for the sun to set, knowing there was only one place he could go for help - and that always led to trouble.

Wood's Harbor is Available now:
Get it Now

Thanks for Reading

Thanks For Reading

If you liked the book please leave a review

For more information please check out my web page:
https://stevenbeckerauthor.com/

Or follow me on Facebook:
https://www.facebook.com/stevenbecker.books/

Made in the USA
Coppell, TX
02 October 2020